# Cash and Carrey

by

R. Orin Vaughn

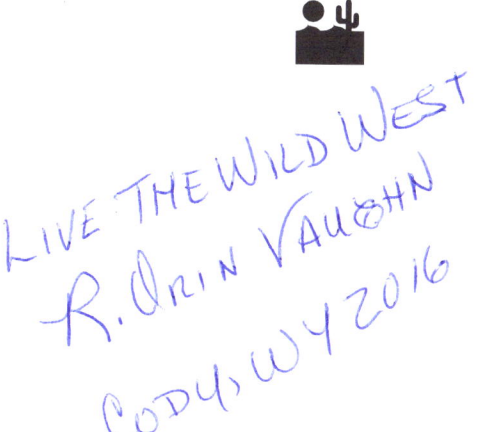

LIVE THE WILD WEST
R. Orin Vaughn
Cody, WY 2016

**Copyright © 2015 R. Orin Vaughn    All rights reserved.**

No part of this publication may be reproduced, stored in retrieval system, transmitted in any form or by any means, electronic, photocopying, or otherwise, without prior written permission of Author. This story is fiction, completely the imagination of the author. Any similarity to actual events or persons is purely coincidental.

ISBN-13:978-1514284230

ISBN-10:1514284235

## DEDICATION

Dedicated to those who have written about the Old West for over one hundred fifty years; to the preservation of the traditional way of Western writing and to the men and women who settled the Western Frontier. To those who, carry on in the Western styles, traditions and ways of life; I say, THANKS. Also, a special thanks to my friend Mike Brose, my wife and family for their support.

                                  Yours Truly,
                                  *R. ORIN VAUGHN*

## CASH AND CARREY
PRELUDE

### Late summer; Ehrenberg, Arizona, 1881

A stiff breeze blows in from the Colorado River as three hardened men on horseback appear out of the darkness, their horses at a walk as they enter town. At the first of a long line of well-lit saloons, the three stop. Each man searches the street carefully.

The first of the three, a big, tall, husky fellow with a full beard that adds menace to his somber expression, dismounts his large chestnut mare and ties it off at a hitching rail. As the man steps up onto the boardwalk, he tucks the tail of his canvass jacket back behind the butt of a .44 holstered at his side. Slowly he wraps his fingers around the pistol. Thumb on the hammer, he adjusts the weapon for readiness.

After tying off his mount the next fellow, a smaller man in stature, searches the street as if expecting someone to jump out of the shadows and grab him. He hurriedly jerks a rifle from the scabbard on his horse and with a quick, metallic-sounding action, levers a cartridge into the chamber.

The last man is tall, lean, with strong weathered features. His straight brimmed hat and long black coat gives him the look of some obscure-out-of-place preacher. Thick, shoulder length, black curls hang down from under the hat. He unbuttons the long coat exposing a precision, blue steel Colt .45

with bone grips, holstered high and butt first on his right hip. The man's movements are sure, yet cautious, a man at his profession. He brushes back his long Calvary mustache with his finger and thumb, then he places his left hand across his belt on the Colt. He taps his finger lightly on the cylinder of the pistol. A slight sinister smile fills the corner of his mouth; he enjoys the familiar comfortable feel of the weapon. It is obvious the man is anxious for the action that is evident to come. Cold, dark blue eyes watch with interest as the husky fellow peers from the shadows over the swinging doors into the first saloon.

The big man at the saloon entrance looks back at his companions and shakes his head. The three move on to the next saloon, the big man on the boardwalks, the smaller fellow walking in the street and the last man still on his mount riding along slowly, repeating their search. They continue the same scenario at the next saloon and then next. Dissatisfied with not finding what they are looking for at the end of the line of saloons, they cross the street.

Each man searches the shadows of the street for movement. At the second saloon on their way back up the other side of the street, the husky man snarls a grin over his shoulder and gives a nod. He has found what they have been searching for; his nod indicates their mark is there. He motions with his hand. The slender man dismounts his horse and ties it off. They each ready themselves knowing what is coming.

Inside the saloon, a smartly dressed young, yet seasoned man, plays stud poker with two cowboys. He is sitting at a table with his back to the bar. From a fine tooled cartridge belt hang a matched pair of nickel plated, ivory handled, .45 caliber Colts. They are quite similar to the precision Colt the man outside is wearing.

The big man and the smaller one enter the saloon quietly, barely noticed by anyone. It is late and only a handful of hard-core gamblers and drinkers still inhabit the place. A barkeep is talking to a cowboy down at the far end of the bar. Interest in the poker game and his senses dulled by strong whiskey, the young man doesn't take note of the two men who have just slipped in. When in position, the two men catch the young man's eye as they stand looking down on him from the other side of the table. He looks up into their menacing glare. "Well, now," the young fellow says as he smiles and pushes back in his chair. "Ned, Lester. How the hell are ya? You fella's just won't give it up, will you?"

"I told you I'd hunt you down no matter where ya run," the big man says.

"So you found me again." A smile forms on the young man's face. "Now," he says, "what makes you think it's gonna turn out any better this time than it did the last?"

Lester, the smaller man, pokes his rifle at the two cowboys sitting at the table. "GEET," he says. The two cowboys sense the conflict, collect their stakes and head for the door; they want no part of this.

The third man, the slim one with the black curly hair, has slipped in. He stands against the bar behind the table about four feet away, unnoticed by the young man.

"You folks see this here wanted poster?" says Ned, the husky fellow, as he pulls a worn and crumpled paper out of his jacket pocket. He holds it up in his left hand for everyone to see. "This here fella and his cousin are wanted for bank rob'ry and murder back in Saw Jaw, Oklahoma. And they even kilt a ranch owner and a woman over in Springerville." Ned stuffs the paper back into his pocket and then steadies himself for the inevitable.

"Where's your hired gun Travis Lambert, this time?" says the young fellow coolly.

"Right behind ya kid," Lambert says. "Ya ain't goin' nowhere this time."

Ned says, "You better hand over them fancy pistols now, Carrey. You ain't got no chance of shootin' your way out of this one."

Lester, the smaller man smiles revealing a mouth full of broken and brown stained teeth and says, "Yep, yer gonna swing at the end of a hangman's rope— Y-e-s sir, ya son-a-bitch."

"I told you boys before, I ain't hangin'. And, I told you what I'd do if you ever called me that again, Lester."

Lester's eyes narrow and his lips tighten as he centers the rifle at the young man's face. "Then I guess you'll die right wheres ya sit," he says.

"Give it up kid," says Lambert from behind as he pulls his pistol and points it at the young man's back.

Lester grins as tobacco drool runs down his chin. The young man's mood turns serious and he speaks straight at Lester and says, "I'll tell you what I'm gonna do, Lester. I'm takin' you with me. And, there ain't nothin' yer brother or that hired killer behind me can do about it, neither."

Lester's expression changes, because he knows the young man always means what he says.

Ned, sensing what is about to happen, goes for his pistol. The young man is fast on the draw even from his awkward sitting position.

Lester doesn't think fast enough to get off a shot before the young man's right hand Colt is out. A shot to the center of Lester's chest sends him stumbling backward a couple of steps as the rifle goes off firing a missed placed round shattering the long mirror behind the bar. Then he slowly sinks lifeless to the floor.

An instant later a shot from the young man's left hand Colt goes wild due to the impact of a slug entering his back from Travis Lambert's .45. The wild shot creases Ned's hair line, but not before he fires a shot point blank into the side of the young man's chest.

The young man goes limp in the chair, his arms drop and the pistols fall from his hands, and with a thud, they hit the floor. The smell of burnt gun powder and smoke lingers in the air.

"LES-TER," calls Ned, blood running down the side of his face and moaning, he goes to the lifeless body of his brother on the floor, and gathers him in his huge arms.

Hugging him tightly, Ned whines to the limp figure in his hands and says, "Dog-gone it boy, what am I gonna tell ma? What'd you have to go and make him mad for? We had him where we wanted him. Damn it anyway, Lester."

A saloon girl, who had just come down stairs as the shooting started, scolds, saying, "You back shootin' bunch of cowards. Cash will be comin' for you."

"That's what I'm a hopin' woman," says Lambert. "In fact, I'm a countin' on it. Where is he anyway?"

"You don't think I'd tell the likes of you?" says the young barmaid as she stands stiff and angry at the bottom of the stairs.

Lambert raises his pistol toward her, aims, it and says, "Yer obstructin' the law here girly. Now tell me where he is."

A frustrated, "Y-o-u, GO to hell," says the girl.

Lambert pulls back the hammer on his .45, his ice cold glare commands an answer.

"He… he went down river with Glenda Wells, the owner of this saloon. He'll be back tomorrow." The young woman's voice quivers, more out of anger than fright, as she continues, "I'd be long gone from here if I was you mister."

"Ya tell him what happened here when he gets back," Lambert says. "Ya tell him, Travis Lambert and Ned Cromwell will be here at two-o'clock in the afternoon, day after tomorrow, to take him dead or alive. That'll give him time to bury his own and think about what he's a gonna do. So, he's got a day to think it over. If he don't get his thinkin' right, he'll end up just like his cousin there. Ya do understand what I'm a tellin' ya, don't ya gal?"

A mean blank stare is Lambert's only answer.

"Ya'all realize," Lambert says, "we're the law. These men are desperados, needin' to be dealt with harshly. We're doin' our duty bringin' them to justice." Lambert holsters his pistol. "Gather up your brother there Ned and let's find an undertaker."

Lambert looks down the bar at the barkeeper and says, "You was smart barkeep not to jerk that axe handle; I'd a killed ya."

"You can bet I'll tell him mister," says the saloon girl. "I'll tell him just how you gunned down Kid Carrey without giving him a chance. That's what I'll tell him for sure."

"Tell 'em what ya want," Lambert says. "Ya just make sure ya tell'm we'll be here for him at two in the afternoon, day after tomorrow. He can come unarmed, or he can come heeled. Either way, don't matter, money's the same." With that Lambert turns and walks toward the door.

Ned bends down to remove the gunbelt from the young man named Carrey. At the sound of a shotgun cocking, he freezes his movements. Ned looks toward the sound. From behind the bar, the barkeep gives a warning gesture with a double barreled shotgun. "Those belong to Cash now. I'll see to it he gets 'em," the barkeep says. Ned nods and goes to his brother. With little effort he bends and hefts him up, slings him over his shoulder to go and find the undertaker.

Lambert, standing by the door starts to back out of the saloon. He reminds the group before he disappears into the night, "Two- o'clock," he says, "day after tomorrow. Tell 'em, don't forget."

The next morning finds Cash, the cousin of Carrey, sitting at a table in the saloon talking over coffee with his close friend, Glenda Wells. "I'm tellin' ya Glenda, it's gonna end right here. There's gonna be a reckoning over this. Ned Cromwell's been a doggin' George and me over that bank rob'ry mess back in Oklahoma, goin' on three years now and I'm gonna end it. I'm tired of running. And now, they've killed George. It's time it was settled once and for all, one way or another.

"We tried to explain to that man, but he wouldn't hear of it. Now he's gonna pay for not listening to our side of it. Him and that no good, crazy, back-shootin', bounty hunter, Travis Lambert. They're gonna pay the price for what they did here last night. Ned should've backed off up in Clifton, took that brother of his and went home. Man just ain't got good sense, I'm telling you. Just won't listen to reason; all he wants is blind revenge."

"What's this all about, Cash?" asked Glenda. "What did you boys do to these Cromwell fella's to make them come down on you like this anyway? And what's the bank robbery stuff?"

"Well," begins Cash, "George and me, George is Kid Carrey's real first name, of course. We're cousins, but... We always been more like, brothers. We grew up together, Glenda..., my...my Ma raised me and George. I mean Kid Carrey... Oh, damn-it. I'm sorry, Glenda." Cash paused as a tear rolls down his face. "A man ain't supposed to have tears like this."

"Now you listen here, Cash," says Glenda. "I've seen lots of men cry over a lot less than this. So, don't you go thinking you're not being a man just because you've got a couple tears rolling down your face. Why, you are one of the manliest gent's I've ever known."

"Thank you kindly for that, Glenda," says Cash. "That's a mighty nice thing for you to say. And you're the nicest lady I've ever known, next to my Ma; a' course."

Glenda smiles, "Of course," she says.

"To go on about George and me," says Cash. He takes a long sip of coffee and begins again, "My Pa was killed by Indians when we were ten and eleven years old. George, I've always called him George. Everyone else calls him Carrey or Kid Carrey since that deal up in Springerville with Mean Gene Green. He liked that tag, seems like every other fella up that way's got some sort of a nickname. Like I said, George is his given name."

"I didn't know his name was George, though that's what you called him all the time. He told me and the other girls to call him *__Kid Carrey__*." Cash stopped and fought to hold back his emotions.

Glenda reached over and held his hand. It seemed to ease him for a moment. She said, "Cash, you alright? You sure you want to tell me this story now?"

"Yeah—yeah, I do Glenda," he says. "I…I've taken quite a likin' to you, ya know, and I just gotta get this off my chest and let someone know the real story. You're easy to talk to, like my Ma was. We ain't talked to nobody about it since we had to leave home back in Saw Jaw, Oklahoma. I gotta talk or I'm gonna bust or something. I wanna tell somebody about George and me now that he's gone. We ain't bad men, it was all just one big misunderstanding, that's all. Now, it's all come to this. I'm gonna even the score with those two, for sure. It's Ned Cromwell's turn to face up to his mistakes. An' dam-it, there's gonna be a reckoning."

"All right Cash, you calm down," says Glenda understandingly. "I kind of know how you must be feeling. Now, tell me about you and Kid Carrey, or George, I guess I should say. Go ahead and tell me everything. I want to hear about how this whole awful mess got started in the first place."

"Well,"—**Cash starts the story**—

# I

George Randolph Carrey's parents died while making the trip across country from Ohio to Oklahoma. They died of a sickness that ravaged the wagon train his family was traveling with. An aunt, my mother, took George as her own and raised him along with her own son, me. I was born Cashes Perry DE White, in '59, and George was born almost to the date, a year later to my aunt. I was about 5 years old, and George 4, when our parents decided to homestead in Oklahoma. George's parents fell short of making the whole trip by about two hundred miles. Almost everybody in the wagon train came down with some unknown sickness. Half the people in the wagon train died from it. George's parents were among the first to succumb to whatever it was; a kind of food or water poisoning some speculated. My mother would never talk about the tragedy and the loss of her sister and brother-in-law. Myself, I hardly remembered the experience.

Instead of homesteading, Perry DE White, my father happened to fall into a deal and started a trading business in a little settlement named, Saw Jaw. The settlement was called that because the first man to build there had used a saw made from the jaw bone of a buffalo to cut timber, or something like that. In just a few years, the trading business was a Mercantile General Store supplying the needs of settlers for miles around.

While bringing in a wagon load of supplies my father and another man were attacked by a band of unfriendly Indians and killed. All they found was the wrecked wagon and the bones of those men picked clean by the buzzards.

My mother ran the store from then on, while George and I helped out. Awhile after my father's death, a panhandler named Pete Drake started coming around about every three months or so. He was pretty sweet on my mother and he took a liking to us boys. We liked him too; he would tell us stories about some of the wild towns he had visited. He collected newspaper articles and dime novels about gunfighters and Wild West characters. George and I loved it when he came around and showed us what he had. We got to read about Kit Carson, Wild Bill Hickok, famous Indians, and the like.

Besides housewares, Drake dealt in and repaired hand guns. He knew a lot about guns and he taught us boys all he knew. He taught us how to shoot and care for guns. We would practice out back of the store whenever we could. When I was fourteen he gave us a .36 caliber Navy Colt to practice with. George and I were out back with that Colt every chance we got, much to my mother's displeasure.

I got to be pretty good at draw and shoot. George on the other hand, had a quick as lighting draw; even fast firing the Colt, he very seldom missed his mark. He practiced fancy twirling and trick shooting. I never went in for the fancy stuff, I just wanted to hit what I aimed at and be able to protect myself should the need arise. I felt confident I could hold my own in a fight.

In April of '79, Ma died. That was a very sad time for the both of us. She left the store to us, and after talking it over, George and I agreed that we didn't want to be shopkeepers, so we sold out.

We thought a long while to make up our minds where we would go and what we would do. Finally, we decided to head out West to California. George wanted to see the ocean so we were going to head for the coast of California where we could see the Pacific Ocean. I didn't really care, as long as it was somewhere West.

We were ready to go, except for drawing our money out of the bank and picking up some provisions. So one afternoon, George and I tied our horses at the hitching post outside of the bank and went inside. The bank was owned by Haden Cromwell, a rich rancher in the area. He helped us withdraw our money that day.

Now, Cromwell had two sons, Ned, a big husky ga-loot over six feet when grown, and Lester, a little fellow that couldn't put his pants on straight unless Ned told him how. We all went through school together and Ned had always been a bully. Lester was slow at book learnin', but would always be there to egg his brother on when he was picking on someone.

One time, George and Ned got into an argument. Ned was teasing this kid with a lame leg and George can't stand someone picking on the disadvantaged. George told Ned to leave the kid alone. After some general name-calling between Ned and George, Ned said the wrong thing. He called George, Georgie Porgy puddin' an' pie. George really hated that. I am probably the only person who calls him George and gets away with it. My mother always called him by his middle name Randolph, which was our grandfather's name.

Anyway, George and Ned went to fisticuffs. George held his own for a while, but Ned was just too big for him. When George realized he couldn't win, he ran and grabbed up some rocks and started chucking them at Ned. That was the end of it for that day.

A few days later, Ned and his brother Lester laid in wait for George and me. They jumped us from behind a building on our way home from school. This time it ended up bein', Ned against me, and Lester against George. It was a pretty severe battle, but in the end George and I came out on top. Though we never fought again, Ned and Lester always held a grudge after that. Lester carries a scar under his eye from that fight till this day.

George and I were never bully types, but George was always ready for a scrap. Except for last night, I have always been there to back him up should the need arise. And with George's mouth, it has seemed to be quite often.

## II

So there we were all ready to head out, except for our business at the bank and picking up a few provisions. George and I went into the bank to draw out our money so we could be on our way. We had three thousand dollars in the bank. We drew out the money and had a brief conversation with Haden Cromwell about us leaving town. Haden was a decent man, just spoiled his sons rotten, is all. Anyway, Haden wished us well and we were on our way out of the bank. In our haste we hadn't given any thought to getting a receipt for the money; had no idea we would ever be in need of one.

As I was about to open the door on our way out of the bank, Billy Joe Tate, another fellow we had gone to school with, came through the door. We said, 'howdy', but Billy Joe just nervously grunted a greeting as he passed. We didn't pay him much mind and went on outside.

Billy Joe and his younger brother Jim were always in some kind of trouble. So when we saw Jim setting on his horse, with the reins to his brother's horse in his hand out by the hitching post, we should have known something was up. We said a greeting to Jim, and got about the same response out of him as we had from his brother inside the bank.

George and I had counted the money while inside the bank and had split it up evenly. We secured the money in our saddle bags and mounted up. Haden Cromwell and a teller by the name of Norman

Croce had been the only two people in the bank to witness our transaction.

We were about to turn and ride over to the General Store when several gun shots, spaced a few seconds apart, came from inside the bank. Right after the last shot sounded, the front door of the bank busted open and out stumbled Billy Joe with a pistol in one hand and a bank bag in the other. He staggered, weak-kneed a couple of steps, and tumbled over the end of the bank porch, dead. Confused, Billy Joe's brother, Jim, went for his pistol. He was gonna shoot at me since I had turned my horse around to face him. Before he could get off a shot, George had jerked his pistol and put him to rest. Jim tumbled backward off his horse and lay in the street.

George and I were fighting our horses to get them under control. They were both rearing up because of all the commotion and noise from the gun shots. Ned Cromwell and his brother Lester, along with a few other locals, came running out of the saloon from across the street with guns in hand.

George and I sure weren't expectin' what was about to happen. We got our horses under control and George slipped his pistol back in place. Ned, and the bunch with him, gathered around us as we got down off our horses. By the time we were on the ground, we had five pistols pointed at us.

"Ya'all boys ain't goin' nowheres. Hand over them pistols and throw up your hands," said Ned.

"Hold on here, Ned," I said. "You don't think we had anything to do with what went on inside the bank there now do ya?"

"All I know is," Ned said, "there's two dead men layin' out here an' one of 'em has a bank bag full of money and I saw you fella's with your pistols drawn. Now, I won't tell you boys again. Hand over them pistols and throw up your hands." Ned cocked his pistol, the others followed suit.

"Lester," said Ned, "go inside the bank and see if the Ol' Man, is alright."

Sheriff Aubrey Brown and his Deputy came up from down the street about that time. "What's the deal here, Ned?" questioned the Sheriff.

"Caught these boys red-handed robbin' the bank, Sheriff," said Ned. The others in the group nodded their heads in agreement. The three fellows with Ned and Lester were just part-time cowhands that hung around to get free drinks. As long as they followed Ned and Lester around and buddied up with them, the well never went dry. Ned and Lester never did have any real friends outside of those they bought.

"I'll be damned if you did, Ned. Sheriff, me and Cash wasn't in on no bank rob'ry. We were here to draw out our money, so's we could take off out west," said George.

"Then how's come you boys had your shootin' ir'ns drawn if you weren't in on the rob'ry?" said Ned.

"I was the only one with my pistol drawn. I had to shoot Jimmy Tate there, cause, he was about to pull the trigger on Cash," George said.

"Y-o-u don't expect us to believe that sorry story do you, Carrey?" said Ned.

"Let's just all settle down here, boys," said the Sheriff. "I'll do the questionin' around here. That's what the County pays me to do."

"Yea, an' my Ol' Man is the one doin' most the payin', Sheriff, an' ya know it," said Ned.

"I suggest you shut your mouth, Ned. I wear the badge, and the citizens of this county elected me to this office. They're the ones that pay my salary, not just your father," the Sheriff said.

About that time, Lester came out of the bank crying and moaning. "The Ol' Man's dead. They killed'm Ned, they killed'm."

"Best you arrest them, Sheriff, or me and the boys here will string 'em up right now. They ain't gonna get away with murderin' my ol' man. I'll see to that, I promise you. They're gonna hang for this."

"Ain't nobody gonna do no hangin' right yet boys." The Sheriff looked at George and me. "You fellas better hand over your six guns, until I can get this cleared up as to what happened here," said the Sheriff.

George was reluctant, but I told him 'we should go along with the law'. I felt Sheriff Brown would see to it that the truth would come out and that we were treated fairly. We handed our pistols over to the Sheriff's Deputy.

"Let's go inside the bank and see if we can sort this thing out. We need to figure out what took place here," said the Sheriff.

Inside the bank, Haden Cromwell lay dead with a bullet in his chest. He was in the middle of the floor face down, and still clutched in his fist was a Hammond Bulldog pistol; the weapon he had apparently fatally shot Billy Joe Tate in the back with, as he attempted to exit the bank. Norman Croce lay dead behind the teller cage; a bullet in his head.

The Sheriff looked at us suspiciously, "Maybe you fellas better tell me what happened here as far as you know," he said.

George started, "Pretty simple Sheriff. Cash and me came in, drew our money out of the bank. On our way out, we bumped into Billy Joe Tate, who was on his way in. Never give it much thought; man's got a right to come into the bank if he's a mind to. We saw Jim settin' on his horse outside, but it wasn't none of our affair what he was doin'. Until we heard the shots from inside the bank, and Jim decided to draw down on Cash. That's when I had to shoot'm. Oh yea, and right before that happened, Billy Joe stumbled out of the bank and fell dead out front there."

"That your story too, Cash?" asked Sheriff Brown.

"Sure it is, Sheriff. It ain't no story, neither; that's what happened," I said.

"Don't believe that for one minute," Ned said.

Lester came in from outside waving our money around saying, "Looky here what I found in their saddle bags. Must be thousands here they stole from the bank."

"We ain't stole nothin," I said. "That money's ours, from the sale of my mother's store. You got no right, just hand it over Lester." Lester stuck it behind his back like a kid hiding candy.

Sheriff Brown said, "Let's not go jumping to conclusions here fella's. These boys said they came in and drew their money out of the bank before all of this happened."

"Okay, I'll give 'em that Sheriff," Ned said. "So if that's so, where's you fella's receipt if you drew your money out?"

"We don't need no dad-burn receipt for our own damned money," said George.

The Sheriff said, "You boys didn't get a receipt?"

"Didn't know we needed one for our own money Sheriff," I said.

The Sheriff looked back on Cromwell's desk. "Deputy, go back and see if there's any information in that open record book on Haden's desk."

The Deputy went back and looked. "It's opened to DE White and Carrey's account alright, Sheriff. But, according to this, they still got three-thousand dollars in their account. Don't say nothing about them withdrawing any money."

"There you go Sheriff. I told you that was a lame story they were a tellin'. Now you gonna arrest 'em or not?"

"Will you shut up, Ned." said the Sheriff; he was getting tired of Ned telling him how to do his job. "I'm afraid I'll have to hold you boys down at the jail till I can investigate this further."

George said, "You can't do this Sheriff. Maybe Cromwell didn't have time to write it down before Tate came in and tried to rob the place. Look here, we ain't done nothin' but draw our own money out of the bank."

"Yeah, that's right Sheriff," I said. "Make Lester give us our money and let us be on our way."

"Sorry boys, can't do that. There's been two men murdered here and I ain't sure about the details yet. You fellas better come along peaceable like down to the jail, whilst I look into this a little deeper. This matter just might have to go to trial," said the Sheriff.

"What, and let them Cromwell boys buy a jury? What about our money?" George said. "You can't let that idiot Lester keep our money." George grabbed for Lester but, he dodged him. The Deputy and another cowboy had to hold him back from causing him harm.

"I'll just have Ned put it back in the bank safe until this thing is settled. Then you boys can draw it out again if you ain't found to be involved in this here hold up business," the Sheriff said.

"Shore, it's gonna be, real safe, in Ned Cromwell's hands," I said in frustrated angry.

"Come on, Sheriff, you've known us ever since you've been Sheriff. You know we wouldn't do nothin' like this," George intently reasoned.

"These are desperate times and I have seen some pretty good men go wrong before," said the Sheriff.

"Don't worry yourself there Cash," said Ned. "You don't need no money when yer swingin' at the end of a rope." With that, two of Ned's friends and the Sheriff had to hold me back from tearing Ned Cromwell's head off. Then the Sheriff marched George and me down to the jail at gun point and locked us up. Needless to say, we were boiling mad about this whole danged affair.

After we were secured in a cell, the Sheriff left the deputy to watch over us. Sheriff Brown left to do more investigating. We didn't see him again until late that night.

He sent his deputy home when he came back to the jail, and put away his gun on a hook near the door. Then he walked over and pulled a wooden stool up to the cell. The Sheriff sat down and said, "I got to say, it don't look good for you boys. I just hope I can keep them from lynchin' you fellas before the trial."

"What are you talkin' about, trial? You know us, Sheriff. We ain't robbed no bank or murdered no one. Come on and let us out of here," I insisted.

"I only wish I could. Those Cromwell boys and there bunch swear they saw you fellas shootin' it up at the bank as you carried money bags out with you."

"That just ain't the way it was at all, Sheriff. They know better than that; them Cromwell boys ain't never liked us. Ther just tryin' to railroad us, an' you know we ain't that sort," George said.

I said, "What about the fact that the bank record book was turned to our account? That's gotta tell you something, don't it, Sheriff?"

"Yeah, I suppose, but I don't know that it's strong enough evidence to dispute eye-witnesses. They got a lot of towns people stirred up, ya know," the Sheriff said. "It just might be up to a jury to decide."

I shook my head. "So we're gonna hang on the word of a bunch of drunks," I said heatedly.

"You boys will get a fair trial, as long as I can keep them from lynchin' you," Sheriff Brown tried to assure us with little or no success.

Certainly, that wasn't much assurance. The Sheriff slept at the jail and he was one sound sleeper, I mean he really rattled the walls when he snored and he snored all night.

Cash and Carrey

## III

Saw Jaw, Oklahoma wasn't a wild town, and the worst criminals that were ever kept in the jail were drunks, so not much attention was given to the upkeep of the jail cells. That night I was in and out of sleep every hour or so, and every time I woke up, George would be at the window in the back wall of the cell, looking out at the night. Finally, I said, "Might as well get some rest George. Looks like we'll be here for quite a spell."

"Maybe you will," said George. "But as soon as I get this last bar loose, I'm gonna be on my way out of here. Come on, give me a hand, but keep it quiet. Don't wanna wake the Sheriff," he said; as if we could, the way he was a sawing logs.

George had all five of them bars broke loose from the mortar. With our strength together, we managed to pull them up and out of the window frame. Carefully and quietly, we laid the bars on the floor. Then we shoved a cot over to the window and climbed out.

Once outside, I said, "What are we gonna do now? You reckon we ought to light-out like this, George?"

"Look here, Cash," George said. "There's a real good chance we'll be lynched before we ever get to trial, if that Cromwell bunch has their way. If we make it to a trial, what do you think our chances of really getting a fair trial are, with them bein' the only witnesses and lyin' on us the way they are?"

I had no choice but to agree with George's reasoning. "Well then," I said, "where do we go from here?"

"Let's sneak over to the livery and see if they put our horses up there for the night."

Staying in the shadows wasn't hard because the only lights in town were coming from the Lucky Duce Saloon; the place across the street from the bank, where the Cromwell boys spent most of their time. We made our way to the livery stables, snuck in, found our gear, and lead our horses out of the corral. When we were far enough away, so as not to be heard, we saddled up.

"What'll we do now George, and how we gonna get our money?"

"Let's ride down the alley next to the Lucky Duce, and see if the Cromwell boys are still there," George said. I nodded and we headed down the back way to the saloon.

We came up beside the saloon, in the alley. It was a warm night, and the windows were open. Staying out of the light and in the shadows, we bent down from our horse, and looked in to see who was in the saloon. The Cromwell brothers and their bunch were just getting up to leave as we looked in. They talked loudly as they exited the saloon and came out on the front porch of the place. We could hear Ned's loud, booming, drunken voice above everyone else's. We could make out some of what he was saying, "All right, Clem. You talk with Wild Bob and Tex tomorrow. Then tomorrow night, we'll drag those murderin' thieves out of that jail, and give them what they deserve at the end of a rope. We ain't gonna wait no month for the Circuit Judge to come in here and let those murderin' sons a bitch's go. That's for sure."

"Looks like you called this one right, George," I said. "What's next?" George turned his horse and we headed back down the alley.

When we were out of ear shot, George said, "Here's what I'm thinkin', Cash, we ought to follow those Cromwell boys home and have a little talk with them. What do you say?"

"Okay with me, let's ride," I said.

From a safe distance behind, we followed Ned, Lester and Clem out of town. They rode straight out toward the Cromwell house. Clem lived with his pa in a cabin up the road from the Cromwell's place, so he broke off a little before they got there.

After Ned and Lester went inside the house, George and I rode up slow and tied our horses off out at the barn. George pulled his rifle out of the scabbard on his saddle, and I did the same. The rifles were the only guns we had since, the Sheriff had taken our six shooters. We both levered our rifles at almost the same instant, so that they made one metallic sound as they chambered rounds ready for action.

"Let's go talk about a lynchin' party," I said.

George nodded and said, "Good idea." He grabbed a rope off his horse and we headed for the front door of the house.

The light from lamps inside shown through the front window as we looked in to see where the two of them were. They both sat at a big oak dining table, as Mrs. Cromwell, their mother, brought them some food from the kitchen.

I signaled George to stand at the side of the door, out of sight. Then I banged on the door with my rifle butt. Ned's voice bellowed. "What'd you forget this time, Clem?" he said. "Come on in, you damned mooch."

I banged again. "Go see what that darn fool wants, Lester," said Ned. "He's always forgettin' somethin'. Maybe he's hungry and wants to mooch a meal."

You should have seen the look on Lester and Ned's faces when they saw it was us, and we had the drop on them. I thought Lester was gonna piss right down his leg.

Ned almost choked on a mouthful of food. Spitting food he said, "You fellas are supposed to be in jail!"

"Well, we ain't. And there's not gonna be no lynchin' party tomorrow night, neither," I mocked.

Lester was as nervous as a man could be. He said, "Ned, H…How'd they get out of j...jail, and h…how'd they know about the lynchin'? What we gon' do now Ned?"

"Shut up, Lester, I don't know. I just know they ain't gonna get away with nothin' like this," said Ned. "Well, if you boys come here to kill us, let's get it over with."

"As much as I'd like to oblige ya, Ned, we ain't gonna kill you right yet. We want our money and we want to know why you fellas wanna lie on us like yer doin'?" questioned George.

Before either one of them could answer, Mrs. Cromwell came in from the kitchen with a big tray of food in her hands. When she saw us, she let go of the tray; it splattered all over the floor. Then she gasped and broke out sobbing with her hands up to her face. In a muffled voice, she sobbed, "What are you two doing in my house? You murdered my husband and that nice little man Mr. Crose. Are you here to kill me and my boys too?"

"We're terrible sorry to bust into yer home like this, ma'am," I said. I really felt bad about having to put her through anymore grief, after losing her husband that day. "Set down here." I pulled a chair out from under the table for her. "Me and George here," I explained, "we ain't murdered no one; contrary to what your sons might have told you. Billy Joe Tate was the one killed your husband and the teller down at the bank. Why, me and George are peaceable fellas for the most part. We just want the money we had in your husband's bank, that's all."

She looked at Ned and said, "Ned, you told me you saw these two rob the bank and shoot your father?"

"Well, Ma," said Ned, "we didn't actually see them shoot the Ol' Man.., I mean Pa. We did see them come out of the bank shootin' and carryin' money bags."

She looked confused over the conflicting stories. It was obvious she wanted to believe her son, so I didn't say any more about it.

"Where's our money, Ned?" demanded George.

"I don't have yer money. It's back in town in the bank," responded Ned.

George was really irritated now, and I didn't know what we were gonna do. Then George took the rope he had brought in, looped it over Ned's head, tightened the knot around Ned's neck. Then he threw the other end over a roof rafter and pulled it tight, lifting Ned up out of his seat to a standing position. "Maybe we're gonna have a lynchin' after all," said George.

I spotted a double door safe by the fireplace in the living room and pointed at it with my rifle and demanded, "What's in that safe there, Ned?"

Ned struggled to talk, as George was keeping the rope taut. Gasping for air, he said, "Just some deeds and personal papers of my Pa's. I don't know the combination, only Pa knew it."

Then Lester gave it up saying, "We *got* the combination, Ned. Member, Pa told us where to look years ago."

Still struggling for air, Ned growled, "Ya just don't know when to keep your yap shut, do you dummy?"

"Don't call him that, Ned Cromwell," Mrs. Cromwell scolded. "He can't help he had the fever and it affected his mind when he was little. If it wasn't for the grace of the Lord, it could have been you, ya know?"

"Yea Ma," Ned said, "I've heard that before. But it wasn't me, and he just let these sons a bitches' know that we have the combination to the safe."

That was the wrong thing for Ned to say. George pulled Ned nearly off his feet and he began to gasp, kick and struggle.

"NED," begged his mother, and said, "Please don't kill my boy." George let go of the rope, and Ned crashed to the floor choking and gasping to get his breath.

"Sorry, Mrs. Cromwell," George said. He pointed at Ned. "Don't you ever call me or Cash that name again. I'll put a bullet in you next time, Ned. Now open that safe, we ain't got all night."

"I forgot where the combination is," said Ned, still coughing and choking.

"You best get to rememberin' real fast, Ned; I'm tired of playin' games with you," threatened George.

"I done told ya; don't remember," Ned held a second time.

George drew a bead on Ned's forehead with his rifle. "Please don't shoot my son. I'll open the safe," begged Mrs. Cromwell.

I really felt bad about being there disturbing Mrs. Cromwell's peace, but Ned and Lester had brought this on themselves.

Mrs. Cromwell went over and fumbled with the lock. The first time she tried, it didn't work. "I'll try again," she assured, and that time it worked.

She stood back, and George went over to the safe. "There's only twelve hundred dollars cash here,"

George said. "You got any other cash in the house, Lester?"

"Only the two hundred dollars Ned's got in his pocket. He won it gamblin' tonight," Lester said. "Oops, I weren't s'posed to tell that, huh?"

"What's wrong with you Lester?" said Ned disgustedly though his teeth, as he rubbed his neck with his hand. It wasn't too awfully smart of Lester to tell us about his brother's winnings like that. Ned was boiling when George made him fork it over.

"Fourteen hundred dollars," said George, "You still owe us sixteen hundred more, Ned. I'll come back and collect it sometime, maybe? How's that set with ya, Ned?"

"Come wearin' yer gun, Carrey. You best kill us right now, cause I'm a comin' after you boys. An' I'll find you wherever you go," vowed Ned.

"Sorry you feel that way, Ned. You know this money is ours. You and Lester were just trying to set us up for a hangin', an' ya know it," I said.

"You two we're tryin' to rob the bank, I know that fer shore. When your partner, Joe Tate, got killed, ya shot Jimmy and made up that lame story about bein' there to withdraw your own money. That's the way I see it," accused Ned.

George said, "Might as well give it up Cash, you ain't gonna convince him of nothin'. He's got it in his head that we were in on that bank rob'ry an' ain't nothin' short of dyin' gonna convince him otherwise. Ain't that right, Ned?"

"You said it yerself, Carrey," said Ned. "And I mean, what I said about huntin' you two down for this."

"Come ahead, if you've a mind, Ned. But let me put you on notice," I assured, "Ain't gonna be no Sunday picnic, cause, we won't go down without takin' ya with us."

"Mrs. Cromwell," said George, "I hate imposin' on you like this, but Cash and me need some provisions before we leave. So if you was to gather some things from yer kitchen an' bring them out in a poke, why we'd be on our way an' not be a botherin' ya no more."

Mrs. Cromwell got up to go into the kitchen. "Oh, Mrs. Cromwell," said George, "don't be forgettin', we got your sons out here." Mrs. Cromwell nodded, acknowledging she understood.

While Mrs. Cromwell was in the kitchen, I took the rope and tied Ned and Lester securely to their chairs. As I did that, George collected their pistols and any other firearms he could find in the house. Beside the two pistols which we kept, George found two shotguns and a rifle. He broke or bent the barrels of all the long guns between two stones in the fireplace, and pocketed the shells and cartridges.

Mrs. Cromwell returned shortly, with a nicely packed flour sack of provisions for us. "Mrs. Cromwell," I said, "before we leave, I want to assure you, that neither George or I shot your husband, or Mister Crose. We were not in on that bank rob'ry, though your sons think we were. Billy Joe Tate is the one that killed those men. Him and his brother, Jim were the ones that tried to rob the bank. George and me were just there getting our money out of the bank like we tried to explain before. I know, you probably believe your sons over us, and I don't hold that again' you; but I just wanted you to hear our side of it." Mrs. Cromwell stared at the floor while I was talking, and afterward she just shook her head. I wasn't right sure what that meant, and I didn't think it good to ask.

Before we headed out, George spoke to Mrs. Cromwell. "Listen now," he said, "we're not gonna tie you up, 'cause it wouldn't be proper, but let me tell you, if you don't want them boys of yers dead, then don't you let them loose from those ropes for at least a couple of hours. We're gonna be watchin' our backs, and if we see'm comin' up the trail; I'll pick'm off with my Winchester. I'm a crack shot, I never miss. You do understand my warnin', don't you ma'am?" Mrs. Cromwell nodded her response.

We both made an attempt to apologize for disrupting her home. Then we told her sons it would be unwise for them to come after us. Ned, again made his threat to hunt us down.

## IV

Outside, barely visible in a pitch black sky, huge, dark thunder clouds were rolling in fast. Occasional streaks of lightening lit up the whole western sky, causing trees and bushes to cast eerie shadows across the landscape, while distant rumblings shook the ground. We knew we needed to ride hard and long; riding into a thunderstorm was gonna to make it rough. The only good thing about it was that a hard rain would make our trail next to impossible to follow.

We rode hard for maybe a half hour before the rains fell. Rain came down in great sheets, pounding the ground as flashes of light lit up walls of pouring water. Loud crashes of thunder shook our very souls. It was a bitter night, worst, I'd ever seen; one not soon to be forgotten.

Though we had our rain gear on, in no time at all, we were completely soaked clear through to the bone. Chilled by the strong wind that drove the rain, we shivered violently. Still fearing the possibility of being followed, we pressed on through the night, always heading west. I'm sure George, same as me, thought of the possible danger of running smack dab, face to face, into a twister. That was a reality we didn't want to dwell on or even mention to each other.

The night was long and perilous; we rode through fast moving, swollen streams; climbed muddy banks and hillsides; and navigated unfamiliar territory. All the while, deafening cracks of thunder rolled over us, and lightning flashed all around. At one point, even set fire to a not so distant lone oak. Still, we rode on through the night.

By daybreak, the rain had let up, not much more than a trickle. By the time the sun was in full view, it had stopped altogether. Birds sang and fluttered in a celebration of the storm's end. The warmth of the mid-morning sun made us feel the drain of the long, hard night's ride. So we held up in an open valley, under a large, old willow tree, in a meadow of prairie grass.

Once great herds of buffalo had roamed this land, as well as tribes of red men living off the land and animals they hunted. Never taking more than they needed, and using every part of the majestic animal for some purpose. Now the buffalo herds were gone, killed off by greedy white men, the Indians confined for the most part on reservations. Sometimes I'm not so proud to be a white man, I thought sadly.

The horses ate grass around the place where we had strung them. George and I ate some biscuits and smoked ham that Mrs. Cromwell had packed in the poke she made for us. George spoke up, first words said since leaving the Cromwell place, "That was one night's ride to remember. Wouldn't you say, Cash?"

"Sure the heck was," I said, as I poured water out of one of my boots. "You don't reckon anyone from Saw Jaw was fool enough to follow us through that storm, do ya?"

"No, I'd hardly think so," said George. "I'm counting on they didn't anyway. But, if they show up, I'm gonna make a stand right here until I can get some rest."

"Me too," I said. "Tell you what, I'll put together a fire and make some coffee. You rest up for a couple of hours, then you can take watch whilst I rest some."

"Sounds like a fair deal," said George, and he slid down low, making himself comfortable, laying his head on his saddle. Then he pulled his hat down over his eyes and was snoring in no time.

I started the small fire, and found a large dead tree limb, big enough for me to sit on. I pulled it over close to the fire. I could sit upright on it so as not to fall asleep while tending the fire and keeping watch.

The sun was high in the sky, directly overhead, when George kicked my foot lightly to wake me. It took a second kick to get me stirring. "Come on, Cash. We've wasted enough time. Let's pack up and get to ridin'," George said, as I sat up and rubbed my eyes.

I felt like I had been run over by the stampede of buffalo I had just been dreaming about. I was so stiff; I think every bone in my body was bruised. "Okay, George, I'm a comin'," I said. "Soon as I make sure I am alive."

We took inventory as we saddled and packed our horses. First town we came across we needed to stop and buy some provisions; we certainly hadn't had a chance to do that back in Saw Jaw.

## V

Outside of stopping at a little no name town for the provisions, we rode steady for the better part of the next three days. Amarillo was the first big stopover, and in the four days we spent there, George found out a lot about himself. He found out he had a liking, for dance hall girls, rye whiskey, cigars and, especially for gambling.

George was a natural at poker; five card stud was his favorite. He even won a pair of fancy, nickel plated, bone handled, Colts in a poker game one night; an outstandingly, Mexican tooled, belt and holster outfit, went with deal. I think the fella George won them from had some thoughts about taking them back. That was, until George took everybody out back of the saloon and put on a demonstration of his expertise with them Colts. George was fast and accurate with those pistols, that's for sure. He handled them like they had been custom made just for him. Why, George could shoot a flea off a dog's tail at fifty yards with either hand with those pistols. He spun those pistols around, threw them up, and switched hands. He did some trick shooting that had the crowd cheering him on. George shot the eyes out of Kings and Queens while some fellow jockeyed the cards back and forth across a rolling clothes line. Wasn't nobody in that bunch that night going to challenge him.

Like I said before, I don't go in for all that fancy gun handling myself. I just want to hit what I aim at and be able to hold my own against any fella who is pushy enough to make me use my gun. There hasn't been a day go by that George ain't practiced with those pistols since he has owned 'em. I have had more than one fella tell me that George is the fastest gun they ever seen.

The next stop on our trek west was El Paso. We had heard a lot about Tombstone, Arizona. Our plan was to head there, and then on to California; however George bought into this horse deal, after playing poker with this fellow named Howard Wayne. The deal was to pay eight dollars a head for these seventy-five horses and we would be able to triple our money by selling them up around Graham County, Arizona.

Sounded simple enough to George; all we had to do was drive them up there, sell them, and be on our way with a pocket full of cash. Thing was, ol' Howard neglected to tell us why he wasn't taking those horses up there himself. No, he didn't tell us about the highway men or the Indians.

So we were off to Graham County to do some horse trading. We made out well along the way, until we got up near to Clifton. Along the way we caught word that our herd would fetch a pretty fair price, if we could get them to Fort Apache; so that's where we would go.

As we lazily guided our herd through an open flat lined on both sides with a thick growth of trees, all of a sudden, we were being charged from both sides by twenty-five to thirty hard-riding-yelping Indians. Naturally, this spooked the herd and they scattered. I yanked my Winchester from the saddle to fire on the attacking band. George swung his leg over his horse's head and slid to the ground, still grasping his reins tight. He pulled and reined the animal to the ground; he had a way with horses, and I think that big sorrel he was ridin' would have done anything he wanted it to do.

By this time, the Indians were firing on us as they circled. They seemed more interested in driving off our herd than really doing us any harm.

George stood ground and both his Colts blazed. Out of two pistol loads, more than a half dozen fast-riding Indians fell. I picked a couple off with my rifle from atop my horse; then a bullet shattered my saddle horn and fragments of it stung my thigh, as the slug spun off singing into the distance. The pack horse I had been leading tried to jerk away and nearly pulled me off my horse. I managed to get him under control and started returning fire again.

The Indians circled round still yelling and firing on us. Most of our herd had disappeared into the thickets; just what the Indians wanted them to do. George had reloaded and was dropping Indians off their horses again. Almost as suddenly as they had appeared, the remaining fifteen or so Indians vanished back into the trees.

George and I were lost as to what to do; we just sat and stood there dumbfounded and numb. In just a few brief minutes, we had lost six hundred dollars in horse flesh; not to mention what we could have sold them for. Our lives, the pack horse, our mounts, and a few dollars were all we had left; and we were dog-gone fortunate to have that.

I caught sight of movement at the edge of the stand of trees. I took aim with my rifle; it was an Indian on a majestic white horse. This was an older, more mature fellow than the braves that had rode in on us. He carried a rifle decorated with rawhide and feathers in his right hand; and if he wasn't a chief or something, he sure looked the part.

"George," I said, "Look. What do you make of that?"

As George took note of what I was pointing at, he readied his pistols again. However, he stopped when the Indian raised his rifle high over his head in what could only be interpreted as a salute or gesture of respect. Then he gave a war cry, turned the magnificent animal, and disappeared into the trees.

"What do you reckon that was all about?" said George.

"Well," I said, "I don't imagine he's accustom to losin' half his raiding party when they attack. I reckon he was letting us know he thought we were worthy opponents."

"Maybe so," George said. "We're the ones that lost all the horses though. I shore don't like losin' the whole herd like that. I don't reckon it would be a good idea to go after'm? Prob'ly couldn't find'm anyway."

"No. We wouldn't even know where we are if it wasn't for the map," I said.

We checked to see if any of the downed Indians were still alive. The first one we found that still had some life left in him raised up and sliced my arm with his knife, as I bent down to help. George shot him as he was about to take another swipe at me. I still have the scare from that knife wound. We found another young brave just barely hanging on. We gave him a sip of water, he took it slowly, and after an appreciative look, he gasped a short breath and died.

George bandaged my arm as we sat pondering what we were going to do. We decided after some, cussin' an' discussin' to go on into Clifton about eight miles away. We sure hated losing the herd, but we couldn't figure a way to recover those horses.

Clifton is a mining town with hard-working, hard-fighting, and hard-drinking men. Having no plan and little money, George and I had no choice but to stick around awhile and see what we could come up with. We hadn't given up the thought of California; we just had to put it aside until we could build a stake to travel on.

Cash and Carrey

## VI

George settled right in gamblin' with the locals, and was building on our stake in no time. Me, I'm no gambler, I never bet on anything but a sure thing. So I got a job working ten, hard hours a day in one of the nearby mines. It was pretty fair money, but I prefer being out and free, sleeping under the stars.

At the Whisky Barrel Saloon where George done most of his gamblin' they had this fighter in a roped off ring every Saturday night. He was a huge muscle-bound fella they called Jacque the Rock; more like a mountain if you ask me. He had long since given up his job in the mines for one as bouncer at the saloon. Ol' Jacque had never been beaten and the Whisky Barrel had a standing offer of a thousand dollars to any man who could stay ten minutes in the ring with him. It cost twenty dollars for a shot at ol' Jacque, and George had tried to goad me into it several times. Thing was, I had no desire to have my skull cracked by that giant of a fella.

Then one Saturday night, when I had a few beers in me and was pretty well fed-up with spending my life in a hole in the ground, I got to thinking; maybe I could go ten minutes with that big hoss. That was after some encouraging words from George, of course.

"You can do it, Cash," said George. "You just stay away from him, and don't let him hit you. Heck, you're fast. Ya might even get in a few licks once in a while yourself. You know, same way you beat ol' Ned Cromwell that time."

So George put up the twenty dollars, and I stripped off my shirt and boots and readied myself for the battle. Then after three other brave lads had lost their hard-earned money, and a few teeth besides, there I was sitting across the ring from big, powerful, Jacque the Rock; waiting for him to beat lumps on my head. I thought, 'How'd I ever let George talk me into this?'

A bell sounded and someone yanked the stool out from under me; I almost fell to the mat. As I looked out over the crowd, I saw a man sitting at a table next to the ring; he was holding a railroad spike over a bell, as he intently watched a stopwatch. I turned to see where Jacque was, and all I saw and felt was that huge fist smashing into my face. I went down hard. Dazed, with blood running out of my nose and mouth, I felt Jacque pick me up and lean me against the ropes to set me up to put me away. The crowd was going wild; there was no doubt they wanted Jacque to crush me out of existence.

I have a pretty hard head though, and wasn't hurt as much as everyone thought I was. I heard George yelling for me to move around, and I thought, 'I ain't gonna give up a thousand dollars this easy'. Jacque was big and powerful, no doubt about that, but he was slow. He drew back that big fist to throw his knockout punch. When he swung, I ducked down, and as I came up, I planted an upper cut into his belly with everything I had. Then I scrambled out from under him to the center of the ring. Jacque was staggered, short of wind; okay, I had dealt him a damaging blow.

When he got turned around and faced me, there was rage in his eyes. "I gonna break you in two for dat," he growled.

I sucked blood through my teeth and spat to the side. "Yeah, well..." I said, "You gotta hit me before you can do that, you big tub." I had my courage up now, and Jacque's punch was just enough to get my dander up too. I figured if I could get him mad, he would lose control and be even more clumsy.

"That's it, Cash," called George. "You got him on the run now," he called.

"Come on," said a dance hall girl on George's arm, screaming encouragements at me.

I motioned with my hand for Jacque to come on, and he obliged. He came at me like a locomotive, full steam. I waited, timed it just right. When he took his swing at me, I ducked, side-stepped a half step, and planted another hard punch to his midsection. Jacque stumbled and fell to his knees. Lack of hard labor for months, rich food, and lots of beer had softened his torso. However, he was up quick leaning against the ropes trying to catch his breath. Half the crowd was now cheering me on, while the rest were booing Jacque. That made Jacque more furious and renewed his determination to crush me.

I looked over at the man with the stopwatch. He was watching the fight; the watch was in his hand face down on the table. I shouted and said, "Hey, you. Watch the time, will ya?" A stocky man in a grey plaid suite, who I recognized as Frank Lutz, the owner of the saloon, took hold of the fellas arm and held it down, as he nodded his head. George was on the other side of the ring, where he couldn't see what was going on.

I yelled at the two of them, and said, "Come on here, you rotten son of a gun. Watch the time." The fella with the watch tried to raise his arm, but Frank held it fast and gave the man a threatening look.

WHOP, a punch to the back of my head nearly knocked me out; Jacque was up and on a rampage. I was on my hands and knees this time when Jacque snatched me up off the mat. Once again, he forcefully set me against the ropes to finish me, and once again I ducked and ran. Only this time I just scramble for my life, no time for an uppercut.

I shook my head and regained my senses; then I led Jacque on a chase around the ring, while I gathered my strength. Now the crowd was booing me. George was shouting instructions from ringside; I was too busy dodging Jacque to make out what he was saying. When I would glance over at the fella with the watch, I saw that Frank Lutz still had his arm. The only way I was going to get out of that ring was on a slab, or beat Jacque. I wasn't sure I could do that, but I had to try. We needed that thousand dollars, and I needed to save my life.

Jacque was close behind me; I stopped, turned quickly, and landed a hard right cross to his jaw. It hardly slowed him down. That wasn't the way I was going to win. The crowd was going wild again, they wanted Jacque to put me away. I had no choice but to work on his weak spot, his stomach.

Jacque landed a few blows and so did I, but none were significant enough to do any damage. I kept Jacque off me by out maneuvering him. I was getting tired, fortunately for me, so was Jacque. I stood backed up against the ropes trying to catch my breath, Jacque came at me like before. I thought, 'it worked before', so I waited till the last split second, right before ol' Jacque took a powerful swing at me. I mustered all the strength I had into one hard, solid punch, side-stepped a half step, and drove it home right into the center of the big man's guts.

P-T-OOF, Jacque spit slobbers out over the ropes, right into Frank Lutz, face. Jacque fell against the ropes; I think they were the only thing holding him up. Then he rolled around facing me, again, I mustered all my strength into one punch and again I sent it home. Jacque's knees buckled, and he grabbed his stomach as he crashed to the mat, face first. He just laid there and moaned.

Frank Lutz shouted vulgarities at Jacque, telling him how worthless he was and how he'd be back in the mines swinging a pick if he didn't get up. Jacque made a halfhearted effort and then collapsed back into the mat. I shouted at the man to ring the bell, but Lutz wouldn't let him do it. Everyone was shouting at Lutz to let the man ring the bell. Lutz looked around at the angry crowd. George was there now, and he told Lutz to let the man ring the bell, or he would be in for big trouble. Lutz took another look around at the crowd, then reluctantly let loose of the man's arm, who immediately struck the bell with the spike. The crowd cheered for five straight minutes, even though I knew some of them lost money betting on Jacque.

I helped Jacque the Rock to his feet. He smiled and said weakly, "You, pretty tough fella. I buy you a drink."

"No, Jacque," I said. "You pretty tough fella. I buy you a drink."

"Okay, dats'a goud too," Jacque said. He grinned big and we both laughed.

When I was out of the ring, on the floor, I walked up to Lutz; George was standing close by. "You owe me a thousand bucks, mister," I said.

"Ha! There was no official time kept, so I don't owe you nothin'."

I pointed to the man at the table, "Only cause you held this man's arm down to keep him from watchin' the time."

The crowd shouting in agreement, "Pay up, Lutz. He won fair and square." Others joined in, "Yeah, that's right," they said.

"No, no, I ain't payin' nothin'. There was no official time, I told you," said Lutz.

Then Jacque stepped up to Lutz and said, "You pay. That man beat me and you gonna pay or..." Jacque drew back his big powerful fist. Lutz went under his coat for an ivory handled, short, barreled pistol. A shot rang out and ricocheted; the pistol went flying out of Lutz's hand. Smoke rolled slowly out of George's Colt, and Lutz was holding his wrist wincing in pain.

"All right, you win, I'll pay up," Lutz said. "I got to get your money out of my safe."

"Don't make us come after you Lutz," said George. "And, Lutz, you come out with another pistol and I'll put a bullet in your head next time."

"I'll be right back. I ain't goin' nowhere," Lutz said.

Jacque, George, his lady and me went over to the bar. We didn't have to buy anything though; everyone else supplied all the drinks for us.

Lutz came back, and reluctantly, handed me the money. Then he told Jacque he was fired. However, no sooner had Lutz said it, than one of the mining captains, offered him a foreman job in one of the mines; he accepted.

George collected another five hundred dollars from bets he had placed on me. Now, we had some traveling money. We were sitting at a table, talking over our plans, when, this well dressed Mexican fella came over. He asked to sit down and talk with us.

"I reckon," said George, "but this kind'a was a private conversation."

"I am sorry, señor. I will only take up a few minutes of your time," the fella said.

"Well, all right. Sit down and have a drink," George said, as he shoved a bottle across the table to the man.

"No thank you, señor," the fella said. "I only drink a little tequila, on festive occasions."

"Well, hell's fire, man," I said, "this is a festive occasion. I just won a thousand dollars. Hey, gal," I called to one of the saloon girls serving drinks. "Does ol' Lutz serve tequila in this place?"

"I think I could round ya up some," said the pretty red head.

"Well, bring it on, and I'll give you a five dollar gold piece," I said.

"You got it, champ," said the redhead.

"No, señor. That is not necessary," said the Mexican fella insistently.

"Aw, come on, mister," I said, "Help me celebrate."

"O-kay señor, I will do that. Just one drink. Thank you," he said humbly.

George leaned forward in his chair and said, "What's on your mind pard?"

"My name is Antonio Diego Martinez. I am here on business; I have a ranch just north of Springerville," said Antonio. "My partner and I have been looking for men such as you, to come and work for us; men who are not afraid to fight and who can handle a gun; men of integrity."

"Well, thanks for the offer and kind words mister," George said, "but, me and my partner are gonna be headin' for California in just a coupl'a days."

"Come on George, let's go up and see the country," I said. "Heck, we got plenty of time to head out for California. I heard the country up there was really pretty. We'll head for California in the spring."

The girl came back with the bottle of tequila about that time. "Pour yourself a drink there, Mister Martinez," I said. "By the way, Mister Martinez, my name's Cashes Perry DE White." After wiping it off on my pants, I extended a hand; Martinez gave a firm handshake. "This here's George Randolph Carrey, my cousin."

As George gave Martinez a half-hearted handshake, he gave me a hard look for telling his full name. "I wanna head for California, now. Don't wanna spend the winter up there," said George, with a school boy scowl on his face.

"Well, I guess that says it, Antonio. Ol' George here's got a hankerin' to see the Pacific Ocean, and that's where we'll be headin' directly. Enjoy your drink and thank you just the same," I said.

"You are welcome, señor. If you should change your minds, the offer will be open for a while. I am leaving in the morning to go back home. If you should come up, ask in town, someone will give you directions to the ranch." Antonio downed the glass of tequila, thanked us again, and left.

George and I polished off the tequila and a beer each, before heading for the boarding house where we were staying.

Next morning, after going down to the livery and getting our horses and gear ready; George and I were walking down the boardwalk on our way to our favorite restaurant, for breakfast. Suddenly, two men stepped out of an alley in front of us to block our path. Right off, I recognized Ned Cromwell, but the other fella, I had never seen before. George and me gave a half a glance at each other and started walking right toward the two of them.

When we stopped about five feet in front of them, the man with Ned sized us up and readied himself; he just stared at us with, stone cold blue eyes. "So, you think yer headin' for California, do ya?" said Ned. "Well, you boys just throw up your hands; you ain't goin' nowheres. Yer under arrest." Ned peeled back his jacket to reveal a badge.

"I don't think so, Ned. Ain't we been down this road before," said George. "Who, was stupid enough to give you a badge, anyway?"

Ned's face burned beet red. He started forward, but the man with him put up his arm and stopped him. "The good citizens around Saw Jaw, Oklahoma wanted Ned to be deputy sheriff. He's come to bring you two to justice; gonna see to it ya hang for the murder of two innocent men."

"And, just who might you be, mister?" I asked.

As if the whole world should know, he answered, "My name's, Travis Lambert. And, I've been hired and deputized, to assist Ned and his brother to bring in the men who killed their father. Now, you vermin hand over them pistols and come along quiet like."

George, not much impressed, said, "Travis Lambert, huh? Sh-ore, I heard'a you. Yer, a back shootin', bounty hunter. So, how ya gonna take us in when we're a'facin' ya?"

Lambert went across his gunbelt with his left hand for his .45, but in a flash the barrel of

George's Colt was in his face. Lambert froze, his pistol half out of its holster.

George grinned wide, "Now, Ned," he said "Ya gotta pick ya a better class of friends than this fella here. I can't believe, the good folks of Saw Jaw really wanted you as deputy sheriff. Ya must'a bought'm with our money. That reminds me, you did bring the balance of what ya owe us with ya, didn't ya?" Ned looked over at Lambert.

"Now," said George, "I'd slip that pistol back into place if I's you, Lambert, and take your hand away. Or, I'll be tempted to put a great big hole right through the center of yer head." Lambert complied.

"From the look on your face, Ned, you don't have our money," said George. "Let me tell you boy's somethin'; we ain't hangin'. We didn't commit no…" The sound of a rifle shot and splintering wood from a nearby post stopped the conversation abruptly. I looked in the direction of the rifle fire and I saw Lester Cromwell across the street, he was fighting with his rifle lever. The rifle had jammed after he fired the shot; it would have hit me had it not been for the post.

"Let's go, George," I yelled, as I turned to run.

George, snatched Ned's and Lambert's pistols and threw them into the street. He followed behind me after firing a couple shots at Lambert's and Ned's feet; causing them to dance and high step it back down the alley. Lester had cleared the jam by then and shot at us, as we ran down the boardwalk. One shot shattered a widow glass close behind us. George stopped briefly, to send Lester ducking and scrambling for cover, by rapid firing several shots with both pistols, splintering wood siding and porch rails all around him.

  We made it to the livery stables, mounted up, and high-tailed it out of there. We had already settled up our account, so we rode straight out of town in a hurry. Again, we were running in unfamiliar territory, with no plan as to where we would go, or what we would do.

## VII

When we had ridden hard and long, far enough that we knew we had plenty of distance, between us and anyone who had followed us, we held up on a high ridge, where we could see for quite a ways off; we talked.

"Well, Cash, where we gonna go now?" asked George.

"I don't know, George," I said. "If we start for California, Ned and them will be right behind us. Someone, must'a told them that's where we'd planned to go."

"I reckon we didn't try to keep it no secret," said George.

"That's for sure," I said. "What say we head up to Springerville and find that Mexican fella? What was his name?"

"Antonio-Diego-Martinez," said George. "That's got some ring to it, ya know. Well, I reckon California will just have to wait awhile longer."

It was about two or three in the afternoon when we rode into Springerville. Sure, is beautiful mountain country up that way. We picked a saloon that looked like it might serve food, and after tying off our horses, we went in.

Smoke hung heavy inside; the place was dark and dreary for as bright as it was outside. There wasn't much going on in the place; a cute, busty, colored, saloon girl sat giggling with a 'dandy' and a ragged looking fella. Three or four cowboys sat around sipping whiskey whilst staring off into nowhere. We stepped up to the bar and asked a burly barkeep with a thick, red, handlebar mustache, if he could rustle us up some grub.

Foul faced and mean, he said, "Beans an' fatback. Fer the both ya. I'l be six bits, in advance."

George smiled and chuckled as he shook his head. "What? No steak?"

"Ain't no damned boardin' house, mister. We serve whiskey here," said the barkeep.

A scowl formed on George's face. "And, you got, a damned quick lip, for a cheap-ass, barkeep," said George.

"Come on George, forget it," I said. "We'll have a couple beers barkeep. Then, we'll find another place to eat, George."

Seeing my point, George let it go. We chose a table nearby, sat down to drink the beer the saloon keeper had drawn for us; that is after I paid in advance. "Dog-gone George, we just got here," I said. "Let's not go stirrin' up trouble right off."

"All right, Cash, but that barkeep had no call to smart, mouth me like that," said George.

"Yer right, George," I said, "but, we don't need to get people riled at us. We might decide to stay around awhile."

"All right, sorry. I'll back off a bit," said George. "I'm just edgy. I don't think I like this town. I wanted to go to California; ya know, see the ocean like we planned in the first place.

"I'm getting' mighty sick of runnin'. I ain't never run from nothin' an' I don't like doin' it now. Hell's far, Cash, we didn't even do nothin' and we're wanted men."

"Yeah, George, I know. I don't like it neither," I said. "But, I don't wanna end up killin' nobody, 'specially if ther wearin' a badge; even if it is Ned an' Lester Cromwell."

Our conversation was interrupted when the 'dandy' got up and started our way. George had a smirk on his face as he watched the fella swagger. I must admit he did look pretty peculiar dressed the way he was. He wore a fancy stitched, black frontier shirt, a red and black pair of Mexican britches, tucked into high, topped Texas boots, with spurs, that had jungle bobs and big rowels that chimed loudly when he walked. And, there was an oversized, bright red, silk neckerchief around his neck, that looked like a babies tucker hanging in front of his chest. A nickel plated, Colt, was holstered on the front of his right hip and a British .44 Adams, was jammed in his belt. A large, bone handled, Bowie knife was strapped to his left side.

He wasn't a big man; he stood not much over five foot, I'd say. When he noticed George looking at him, he stopped at our table. He was an older fella, with shoulder-length, grey-black hair and bushy eyebrows. He spoke through a mustache, that grew down and covered his mouth. He addressed George and said, "You got somethin' you wanna say fella?"

I took a tight grip on George's arm, "Let it be, George," I said.

George complied, for a change, which surprised me. He said, "Me? No mister, I ain't got nothin' to say."

"Good," is all the 'Dandy' said. Then he went on out the back door of the saloon. I reckon his business out there demanded first attention.

George shook his head. "Now, that's somethin' Cash," he said. "I ain't never, seen a fella dressed like that before."

"I ain't neither," I said. "Sure got a mean look about him though."

I ordered another round of beer and had just taken a sip, when a fella pushed open the saloon doors. He stood in the doorway for a moment, looking around, and adjusting his eyes to the dim light. He was a tall, slim, young, colored fella, wearing Army pants with a yellow stripe down the side. He wore suspenders over a faded flannel shirt and a cavalry hat topped him off. An Army Colt, hung in a cut down Army holster, on his side.

He spotted the saloon girl sitting with the ragged fella, and walked over, sat down with them. He leaned over and whispered something in the girl's ear, she smiled.

The shabby fella, wasn't happy about this newcomer. "Ya'd better git on out'ta here," he said. "Mean Gene Green, is'a entertainin' the lady. An' he'll kill ya fer shore, when he gits back, if'n yer still here."

"Best listen, boy," said the barkeep.

"Mean-Gene-Green, huh? We-ll, I'm pretty damn mean myself." The young fella, boldly stood up and said, "In fact, I can lick any man here. Anybody wanna try me?"

George and I looked at each other. George smiled and said, "Go ahead Cash, you're the boxer."

"Heck, George, I don't wanna fight nobody. I just wanna drink my beer and get somethin' to eat. Then we'll look up Martinez."

The young fella strutted over to a cowboy sitting at a table by himself. "How 'bout you cowpuncher? You wanna try me?" He leaned down in the cowboy's face and bellowed saying, "I'll, rip yer heart out and eat it. I did that to an Indian I killed once. Come on cowboy, you look tough."

The man looked up from his drink, shook his head, then went back to his drink.

"See that," said the young fella. "These people know, I'm hateful and mean. They know better'n take me on." With no takers, the fella sat back down and talked with the girl; she giggled about whatever it was he was saying.

We didn't think much more about it until the 'dandy', the so called, Mean Gene Green, came back into the saloon. When he saw the man sitting with the girl, you could see he was none too pleased with that. Mean Gene stood by the bar and the barkeep said, "He says he's mean. Can lick anybody in the place."

"Humph," snorted Mean Gene. He pulled the .44 Adams out of his belt and put his hand behind his back hiding the pistol. Then he walked over to the table. "Say you're mean, huh? Ya want that on your gravestone?"

The young fella looked Mean Gene up and down, leaned back in his chair and locked his fingers behind his head. He smiled big, and chuckled saying, "I suppose, yer Mean Gene Green. I ain't impressed much, Gene."

Mean Gene said, "Yer dead, BOY."

The young man's smile change to an expression of rage, as he unfolded his hands, obviously, being called boy, was something that offended him. Without warning, Mean Gene brought around the .44 Adams from behind his back, and blasted the young fella right in the face. The chair went crashing back to the floor, leaving the young man sprawled out on the floor. The saloon girl screamed at the gory sight of the young man. The shabby fella cupped his ear with the palm of his hand. No doubt, the sound of the Adams going off, so close to his head, had smarted pretty good.

Mean Gene, turned as smoke drifted out of the barrel of the .44; Gene, put the barrel up to his mouth, blew away the smoke, then spun it backward in his hand and slipped it back into his belt. Mean Gene, shrugged his shoulders and said, "He went for his ir'n. Wasn't, nothin' else for me to do, but defend myself."

Still holding his ear, the ragged fella stood up and said, "'at's right. 'at's the way I see'd it. The black drew first."

"That's good, Dirk. Now, sit, an' shut up," said Mean Gene. He walked our way. "Ye'all saw it that way, right?" He looked at us, "Ain't that right, you two?"

"That young fella, didn't draw at all. That's the way it was, and that's the way I saw it," said George. Mean Gene stopped, gave George a hard look. George, loosened himself, and flexed his fingers.

The barkeep, spat tobacco at a nearby spittoon, and said, "The…the black drew first." I don't think the barkeep wanted anymore gunplay in his saloon for that day; it was a pretty messy sight. "That's the way, I seen it Gene. Let's not have no more killin' in here today.., okay? It ain't good for business. Come on Gene, drinks on the house."

"You know, kid, al'm startin' not to like you," Gene. "But, I ain't gonna kill ya today. I'll save it for another time."

"Ain't our fight, George," I said. "Let's go get something to eat."

"Alright, Cash," answered George. "Let's go, before, I lose my appetite."

Mean Gene, went back to his seat, grabbed the saloon gir, pulled her close, and kissed her on the mouth; she didn't like it, but she gave in, having little choice. He told the ragged fellow, Dirk, and one of the cowboys in the saloon, to carry the dead man outside. Gene, then broke open, the .44 Adams and started cleaning it with a cloth.

As we walked by Mean Gene, he said, "Another time, kid."

"Count on it," said George.

After leaving the saloon, we found a homey looking restaurant down the street, and went inside. George and I, sat at one of the long tables, with bench seats; a lad, I guessed to be, twelve or thirteen years old, introduce himself, as Eric. He said, 'they had the best steak in Arizona' so, we ordered steaks, with all the fixin's.

As he set the table, I asked, "Hey son, you know how we can get to the Martinez ranch?"

Eric's eyes opened, wide as saucers, he paused, "You…you'd, better ask my mom about that, mister," said the boy. "I don't think, I should say, sir. I'll go back and get her."

George looked at me, "Wonder what's that about?"

I shrugged, "You got me."

Shortly, a woman came out from the kitchen in quite a stir; she stood at our end of the table, eyes wild and flashing. She wiped her hands on her soiled apron; strands of dark brown hair, hung down in her even darker brown eyes. Unsuccessfully, she tried to blow the hair out of her face with her bottom lip, as she threw her head to one side. She, sharply, glared into George's eyes, and said, "Can't you people, leave those folks alone? They're only trying to make a living, like, everyone else around here. Just leave them alone? Haven't, the likes of you, done enough, to make their lives miserable?"

"Hold on here, ma'am," I said. "We ain't here to cause any trouble. Antonio Diego Martinez invited us up here to come work for him."

Embarrassment filled the woman's face. "Oh…I thought.., you were here.., Well, never mind," she said. "I am sorry. I mistook you for hired gunmen."

"That's all right, ma'am. Yer, kind'a pretty when yer angry," said George as he pushed his hat back on his head and took careful note of the woman.

She smiled and her dark, almost black eyes, sparkled shyly as she said, "Thank you for the compliment, I think. If you're really going to work for Mister Martinez and Johnny Grey-Wolf, I suppose, I could tell you where their ranch is. You are sure, you're going there for a job? You're not working for Eli Gustafson or Rance Logan."

"Right now we ain't workin' for nobody, ma'am," I said. "I can't say for sure we'll take it on but, we're goin' out to see what kind'a job Martinez has in mind."

"Well," the woman said, "I just can't understand why, all the ranchers can't give up a little space, and get along instead of fighting all the time. I am sorry that I came out here and made such a scene. I suppose, it really isn't any of my business, but I just don't approve of settling things with a gun. I mean, it seems, every time you turn around anymore, some fella is getting shot down in the street. It's just plain sorrowful. Mister Martinez and Johnny Grey-Wolf and their families are good, hard working, people. They deserve to be treated better than they have been by folks around here. Well, anyway, I'll have your meal out in here in a few minutes. I'll let you have a piece of my peach cobbler, on the house, for the way I jumped on you fellas."

"That would be real nice ma'am," George said. "Peach is my 'very' favorite." The lady turned and went off to get our food.

I raised an eyebrow and said, "Since when is peach, your 'very' favorite, George? You've always liked apple the best, ever since I've know'd you. And, I've known you a damn long time."

"Well, peach is good too. I mean a fellas taste can change over the years, you know," said George.

"I don't think it's yer taste in cobbler that's a changin'," I said. "I think, you got an eye out for that pretty little gal."

"Me…Her? Naw, not my type," said George. "She don't appreciate shootin' ir'ns. I think a pair of pistols, is the only way you can settle things once and for all in this country. I'll hang mine up when everyone else does, an' not until. Really though, it seems to me that most women just don't understand that."

"A fella don't have much choice," I said. "If ya don't go packin', yer beggin' for some low down to take yer head off, without a second thought; just like that young fella, ol' Mean Gene killed."

The boy and his mother came out with our meal. And, one fine feed it was too. After we finished the steak and all, the woman kept her promise, and brought out two large bowls of hot cobbler, with fresh cream on them. It just melted in your mouth, it was the best meal that George and I had since my mother died.

If the way to a man's heart, is through his stomach, then George was hooked all the way, and the lady wasn't a bad looker neither.

As we finished devouring the cobbler, the woman brought out the coffee pot and sat down on the bench across from George. She poured our cups full and said, "I am sorry, we got off on the wrong foot, fellas. My name is Lydia, Lydia Price." She extended a hand and shook both our hands. "My mother-in-law, Gracie Price and I, run this restaurant. My son Eric, helps when he's not in school."

"Nice to know you, ma'am," I said. "My name's Cashes Perry DE White and this is..." I looked over at George. "You tell her your name George. Heck, I don't know how I'm supposed to iner'duce you."

George laughed and Lydia looked puzzled. "My name is George Randoff Carrey," he said, "Most just call me Carrey."

"You always get upset when I iner'duce you like that," I said.

George didn't even hear me, he was too spellbound with Lydia. "Where is Mister Price, Lydia?" said George.

"Not with us anymore. A few years back Eric was killed by a man they call, Mean Gene Green in a saloon fight over a card game."

"We're sorry to hear that," George and I said.

"Oh, I am sorry he is dead too, I guess. But, he was never much help to us anyway. Always gambling, drinking and fighting. He never wanted to work or help us run the business. Mrs. Price, my son's grandmother and I have never really let young Eric, know what a no-count his father was. I'm worried about him though; Eric says he is going to get, Mean Gene Green someday, for killing his father."

"Lydia?" George said, "That's a Bible name, from the New Testament, ain't it?"

"Why, yes it is," Lydia said pleasantly. She was impressed with George's comment. George and me were some familiar with the Bible. My mother used to read it to us every night before bed when we were younger.

"My father was a Baptist Preacher back east," said Lydia. "He named all us girls from the Bible. I have four sisters back in Pennsylvania. I was a foolish young girl, and ran off with my childhood sweetheart, who turned out to be a drunken bum. That was my son Eric's father. My husband's mother, came out to be with her only son after her husband died. She had a little money, so she opened this restaurant. I have helped her run it from the very start. She gave me half ownership when her son was killed."

Seemed Lydia, had taken an instant liking to George. She dog-gone near told us her whole life story, right there and then. Eric, her son, came out and sat down with us after a while, he had all his chores done. After we had drank the whole pot of coffee she said, "Well, I have talked long enough, I guess I had better tell you where the Martinez Ranch is, so you can be on your way."

After she gave us the directions, and an invite back for breakfast, George asked about a hotel. We had decided to wait until morning, before riding out to the Martinez ranch.

We stabled our horses and registered at the hotel. I looked around town a bit while George found a poker game at a nearby saloon. Shortly, I turned in for the night. I was pretty well worn, when I hit the bed and I didn't hear George come in that night.

I was up early the next morning, George didn't even stir when I left the room. I sat in a chair, leaned back against the wall on the front porch and enjoyed the morning and hotel coffee. I don't think, George came down until almost eight o'clock. After a hardy breakfast at the restaurant, Lydia was too busy to talk and only smiled and said "Hi". We headed for the stable to get our horses. As we approached the saloon, where we had met up with Mean Gene Green, the day before, the doors slammed open and out rushed, Mean Gene and his shadow, Dirk. They didn't notice us as we came up. They were too busy watching some fellow walking down the street.

"I tell ya Gene, 'at's one of dose 'ere fellers what got a half dozen or so wives to 'imself," said Dirk.

"You shore?" said Mean Gene. "That jess ain't right, you know. Let's see if a bullet will pass right through'm like some say."

"Yep," said Dirk, "'at's what a feller done told me, here while back. Sar it happen, up in Utah."

With that, Mean Gene slowly drew the Colt out of his holster and took aim at the fellow walking down the street. The man in the street wasn't even armed.

"HEY" called George, from behind Mean Gene. "What, the hell? Ya, plum damn crazy, or what, man?"

The man in the street looked to see what was going on. When he saw the pistol aimed his way, he ran for cover and ducked out of sight, behind a water trough. Mean Gene, turned and faced us and said, "You again pisser? You got a big mouth, and you got a bad habit of stickin' yer nose in, where it don't belong.

"Mighty fancy set of pistol you got there kid. They jess for show, or do you know how to use them, pisser?"

George said, "Ther's only one way yer gonna find out, Genie, ol' boy."

"Mean Gene done went an' kilt 'imself, mebee.., tin, twelve men countin' 'at black here yes'erday," said Dirk.

"Is that a fact," said George. I didn't interfere with George this time. I did, however, stand ready just in case, Dirk had thoughts of getting in the gun play.

"What's yer name kid?" asked Gene, as he slipped the Colt back in its place. I'm pretty sure, he said and did that as a distraction.

"I'd like to know what yer called, before, I make ya number thirteen."

"Carrey," said George, "Ya all talk, Genie boy? Or, are you gonna make yer move? Just don't think thirteen's gonna be yer lucky number today."

"Kid.., Carrey. You want that on yer gravestone, pisser?" Gene went for the .44 Adams in his belt. Apparently, this had worked for him many times, but not today.

In half a blink-of-an-eye, both of George's Colts blazed; two shots from one, and one shot from the other. Mean Gene Green stood, weak kneed, with a confused look on his face, the Adams half raised. Gene's face went blank, as he squeezed off a shot into the boardwalk, and wilted to the ground where he lay dead, with three .45 slugs in his midsection.

George stepped over Mean Gene's motionless body, and with a sinister scowl on his face, put both his pistol barrels to his lips and blew away the smoke. He then spun the pistols in his hands and planted them firmly back into place. George said, "He went for his ir'n. Wasn't nothin' I could do, but defend myself. Want that, on yer damned gravestone."

Dirk, stood dumbfounded for a minute, then went running down the street shouting, "Kid Carrey, done went an' kilt Mean Gene Green…Kid Carrey done went an' kilt Mean Gene."

George smiled and said, "Kid Carrey? I think, I kind'a like that." So George was tagged, Kid Carrey, from that day on. Like, most every other hombre, up around that area, he had himself a nickname.

The fella that Mean Gene was about to gun down, when we happened along, came up to us. "I want to thank you, mister," he said. "That stupid fool, would have shot me down in the street, if you hadn't stepped in. I don't know what made Green target me, or why you took up the fight, but I sure am grateful."

"Dirk said somethin' about you havin' a half dozen wives and bullets passin' through you; that's when, Mean Gene drew down on you. Me and him weren't on too good of terms anyway," said George. "I wasn't gonna stand by and let him gun down an unarmed man. I hope the local law will understand that."

"Me, I'm not even married yet, and I certainly ain't of a religious nature. Don't worry about the law," the said. "The county sheriff is up in St. Johns, and the deputy is a good friend of my family. Nobody's, gonna care much about Green anyway.

"I always, leave my rifle in the wagon, when I come in town for supplies, and I never carry a hand gun. By the way, my name is, Timothy Logan." The fella offered a hand, and, when I shook hands with him I realized he was no ranch hand; hands too soft, and no sign of calluses. "You fellas can call me, Tim, of course."

"Logan?" said George as he shook hands. "Where have we heard that name before, Cash?"

"Lydia, said somethin' about, a Rance Logan, last night," I replied.

"Yes, Rance Logan is my father," Tim said. "Our family has half ownership, in the GL7, Cattle Company."

"GL7?" I asked.

"Yes. GL, stands for Gustafson and Logan," said Tim.

"Oh, I see," said George. "We're pleased to meet you. I'm Kid Carrey, and this is my cousin Cashes

DE White. You can call me, Carrey, if you want, and he mostly answers to Cash."

"Sure. Nice to know you fellas. Listen," said Tim as he shook my hand, "I'd like to have you fellas come out to our ranch and meet my family. We'll roast a side of beef and introduce you around. You fellas, are going to be around awhile, aren't you?"

I look at George, my eyes fixed and brow raised; he ignored my look and said, "Shore. We'll be around awhile. We got some business to look after, that will keep us around for a least a few weeks, anyways. We're staying at the hotel. You can leave a message for us there."

"Great," said Tim. "I'll make the arrangements, and get back with you at the hotel, real soon. Well, I got supplies to buy. I thank you again for stepping in and saving my hide." Tim nodded and was on his way.

I said, "You really think that was a smart thing to do, acceptin' an invitation out to his ranch like that?"

"What's the harm," said George. "We ain't takin' no sides in this deal. We don't even know what's goin' on for sure."

"Well, I reckon that's true. I just don't want to get in the middle of some feud between cattlemen. Heck George, we got enough of our own problems to deal with, like, Ned, Lester and that other fella, what's his name…Lambert? We don't need to get caught up in nothin' else."

"Ya worry too much, Cash," said George. "We ain't gonna see nothin' of Ned and Lester again. They'd be plume dumb to trail us any further."

"Maybe so George," I said, "But, I didn't expect to see them in Clifton either."

"You got a point there, I s'pose," said George.

"Let's get someone to get this fella out of the street," I suggested. "Then we'd better get on out to the Martinez ranch." George agreed, and we found an undertaker. George paid for Mean Gene's burial; after that, we gathered our horses and left town.

## VIII

It was a beautiful ride out to the Martinez ranch. Tall, majestic, pines lined the trail, distant hills and mountains, touching a clear, blue sky, that would be hard to match anywhere.

When we arrived at the gate, something didn't seem quite right, with the place. I couldn't put my finger on it, at the time, but it just didn't have the feel of a cattle ranch. There were, two adobe houses across a cleared lot, from one another. One looked fairly new, fresh built, while the other had some age on it.

We stopped in front of the newer house, and were almost ready to dismount, when the door opened. Out rolled an Indian man, in a wheelchair. A pretty, dark skinned, young girl, with long black hair was pushing the wheelchair. A polished, well cared for Springfield rifle, lie across the man's lap. His finger was on the trigger, and, his thumb was on the hammer, ready to use it in short order.

"You leave this land. We will, defend ourselves," the man said.

"We ain't here to cause no kind of trouble mister. We're lookin' for, Antonio Diego Martinez. We were told this was his spread," said George.

"His, and mine. What do you want with him?" said the Indian man. The girl, stood silent behind the wheelchair, with one hand on the chair and one on the man's shoulder.

"He offered us a job while we were down in Clifton," George explained; his patience was starting to wear thin. He didn't take to telling strangers his business.

"I do not believe you," said the man. "You are working for Eli Gustafson. Come here, to run us off our land." The man's black eyes glared cold and his hands tightened on the rifle.

I said hoping to lighten things up a bit, "That's about a 42 Model, Springfield Musket, ain't it?"

The Indian's face relaxed a some, but it didn't work long. "Yes it is," he said proudly. "My father hunted with it. And, when he died it was given to me."

"Ya must be Johnny Grey-Wolf," I said.

"Yes, I am John Grey-Wolf. Enough talk. I want you off our land." The hammer on the rifle clicked as it came up and fixed in on George. It was pretty obvious that, Grey-Wolf didn't take to George none. George's hand was to his right hand Colt. Just a heartbeat, before the shooting started, a familiar voice from behind us, broke the unnerving silence. Someone had come out of the other house.

"Wait John," a voice called. "I know these men. I asked them to come up here. I did not think they would come, but they did." It was Martinez.

"You know them well enough to know they do not work for, Eli Gustafson or Rance Logan?" asked John Grey-Wolf.

"Si. Not these two," said Martinez. "They would not work for such a man as Eli Gustafson, or his family."

"Well, maybe I misjudged these two," said John Grey-Wolf, as he rested the musket back across his lap and set the hammer. "But, we do not need help from outsiders. We can handle our own affairs."

"Handling our own affairs, my friend, is what put you in the wheelchair," Martinez said.

John Grey-Wolf, threw up his hands and said, "Do what you want then." He motioned for the girl to take him back in the house. As she turned him around, he said, "Just, do not come to me, when they turn out to be trouble."

Martinez, directed us toward the door of the house he had come out of, across the lot. As we walked toward it he said, "John Grey-Wolf, is really a good man. He is just bitter about what happened to him."

"What did happen to him?" I asked.

"Come into my home," Martinez said as he opened the heavy, wooden, iron hinged door. "I will explain everything to you, as my wife gets us something to eat."

Once inside, Martinez introduce us to his family saying, "This is my wife Juanita." She was a proud elegant woman with beautiful dark features. Martinez continued down the line, starting with his oldest son, Hector. I would say, he was just a little younger than, George and me. Then, Antonio introduced, his oldest daughter Antoinette, she was sixteen or seventeen. Next, was Conchita, about thirteen. Finally, Ramon his youngest, probably eleven or so.

"I am sorry, señior's, I must apologize. I have forgotten your names," Martinez said.

"I'm, Cashes DE White, most just call me, Cash. And this is my cousin, Geo...," I paused, then said, "Oh heck, George, I never know what to call ya anymore. Tell these folks, what ya want them to call ya."

"You can just call me, Carrey," George said. "It's nice to meet yer family and all, but, to just get to the point; what kind of job did you have in mind for us, Antonio?"

"Well, my friends," said Martinez, "about six months ago, John Grey-Wolf my partner, was out mending fence that had been deliberately destroyed, which has been happening more and more often in the last year. Three of Gustafson and Logan's men came up on him by surprise, grabbed him, and threw him off a twenty foot cliff. Good for him, he landed in some soft dirt; however, his back was injured, so that he cannot walk. That is why, he is in a wheelchair. I knew then, we needed capable help, from men such as yourselves. Knowing, I would not find such here, I went to Clifton, hoping to find someone willing to be hired and help. I talked to many, and you were the last I talked to. No one was interested in coming, that is why my heart was glad, when I saw you were here."

"So, you're wanting hired guns for revenge, or something like that?" said George.

"No," said Martinez. "Nothing like that. What we need is, men who are not afraid to work under the possible threat of men like that of Eli Gustafson, and Rance Logan. Men, who will watch over our herd and protect them."

"Well, we ain't cowpunchers, Mister Martinez," said George.

"We are not cattlemen," said Martinez. "We are Sheep-herders. That is why we have fenced around our ranch, to keep our herd in and cattle out."

"Oh, I see. Sorry, Mister Martinez," George said, "We ain't gettin' involved in no damned range war, over a bunch of sheeps."

"Hold on a minute, George," I said. "These folks need help. It ain't like you to turn down people in need."

George said, "I don't mind helpin' people in need, but, I ain't getting' in the middle of no fussin' over dumb animals, or people arguin' over the height of prairie grass. Besides, wasn't it you who said, we shouldn't get in the middle of any feuds."

"Well," I answered, "I guess maybe I did but, that was before I knew how desperate this deal was." I was a little disappointed in George's attitude. "No matter what, I said before, I aim to do what I can to help these folks out. I mean, nobodies got a right, to cripple a man over makin' an honest living in hard country."

George frowned and said, "Hell's far, Cash, ya don't even know what ther gonna pay ya, to risk your life an' limb. You'd better think about what yer commentin' to, before ya pull the trigger on this deal."

Martinez said, "We will pay you more than the usual hired hand."

"There ya go, a little more than the average sheep-herder. That shore is one hell'a deal, Cash."

"It ain't a matter of pay," I said. "Good folks, need help, and by god, I'm gonna do my damnedest."

"Okay Cash," said George, "but you will, forgive me, if I don't join you, this time. I'm gonna set this one out."

"All right, George," I said, "You do what you thinks right, and I'll do the same."

"Look here, Cash," George said, "don't get yerself, thrown off no cliffs, and make me come out here and kill somebody."

"I'll do my best but, without you to watch my back, I'll have to take extra care," I said.

"I'll still be around, to deal with any serious trouble," assured George. "Ya just do yer best, to keep it down to a skirmish, instead of a full scale war."

"When do I start, and where do I sleep and stow my gear?" I asked Martinez.

"We have a bunkhouse, behind the house where, John Grey-wolf's nephew, Ira, stays. He is out on the range watching the herd and mending fence," said Martinez.

"Well, if it's good with you Mister Martinez, how 'bout, I come out ready for work, Monday mornin'. That will give me a few days to look around town and get familiar with the territory?" I said.

"It will be very good to me," said Martinez.

## IX

We stayed, for a great supper, that Misses Martinez made, then we said our thank you and good-byes, before heading back into town. George was unusually quiet on the way back and I didn't mind, cause, I wasn't much on talking either. George and me seldom disagreed but, this time, we just didn't see it eye to eye.

When we got back to the hotel, we found that Tim Logan had left us a note, inviting us to come out to the GL7 ranch the next day. He wanted us to come around noon and meet family and friends. He mentioned in the note, about preparing a side of beef and that he especially wanted, Kid Carrey to meet somebody named, Vern. There was also a map with directions, showing us how to get there; it looked like about an hour leisurely ride from town.

After looking at the message, I mentioned, "I ain't sure it's a good idea we go out there."

George gave me a hard look. "Yeah, we should," said George. "We need to see the other side of this deal. Maybe, you'll see the sense in, stayin' out-ta this thing; if ya see how strong the feelin's of both sides are. Besides, I went out to Martinez's with you, so's you'd better damned well go with me out to the GL7."

"Well alright George," I replied, "If ya feel that strong about it, shore I'll go. That's what we'll darn well do."

George relaxed his demeanor and said, " Thanks Cash. I appreciate that. I hope you don't hold it again' me for havin' a different way of thinkin' on this. I just can't go up against trouble, I don't feel I have no business buttin' into."

"Like I said before, no hard feelings. You do what you feel is right, and I'll do the same. Just don't set around here though; go make some money for our poke, gambling or something," I said.

"I can shore enough handle that Cash," George said.

"Good," I said, "We'll head out to the GL7 ranch after breakfast then."

Next morning, because of George's insistence, we found ourselves eating breakfast at the Price House Restaurant. When I mentioned to George that, we were going there so he could see Lydia, he firmly denied it and said he wanted to go there because they had good food, 'Yeah sure George' I thought. Though they did have good food, it was pretty evident, that there was a developing passion between the two of them.

After we ate, and, the breakfast crowd died down, almost a whole pot of coffee, a long conversation with Lydia, and a dish of peach cobbler with cream, we were finally on our way out to the GL7 ranch. It was near ten o'clock when we left town.

A mile or so out of town, we found rolling hills, with few trees, and lots of flat land with high grass. By the time we arrived at the GL7 gate entrance to the ranch, the sun was high in the sky, and it was getting uncomfortably warm.

After going through the entrance, it was another half mile to a huge log ranch house that sat with a barn, corral and small bunkhouse. It all was all setting peacefully on about an acre and a half of cleared land; except for two huge cottonwood trees for shade. There were five or six horses loose in the corral and two horses under saddle, tied at one of the two hitching rails at the ranch house. As we rode up to the house, two men came out the door of a little structure built off the side of the barn, carrying a side of beef on a stretcher; one had a large butcher knife in hand with the stretcher handle. They headed for a spit, set up with firewood, about twenty yards away. They stopped frozen when they spotted us, giving a hard quiet stare; after, an uncomfortable period of silence, Tim came out from the ranch house, all friendly and laughing a greeting. Not until then, did the two men relax their manner and continue their way out to the spit, where they set the stretcher down and started the fire going.

We dismounted and tied our horses at the house hitching rail with the two already there. We were barely off our horses, when Tim embraced us hardily, thanking us for coming. He told us, we were the first to arrive and that his father, brother and Vern were out doing some branding but, should be home shortly. Tim invited us to sit on the porch and enjoy a glass of lemonade, while we waited on the other guest.

"Mei-Li," *(May-Lee)*, Tim called into the house, "Bring out a pitcher of lemonade, and three glasses please." We all sat down and shortly, a middle aged Asian woman, brought out the lemonade and poured it for us and then returned to the house. As we sat talking and sipping lemonade, we learned a lot about the back ground of the GL7 Ranch and the people who owned and ran it.

Rance Logan, Tim's father was Eli Gustafson's nephew; he had come to Arizona from Chicago and bought the ranch, with money, he had mostly borrowed from his uncle, Eli. Rance, had started out with just two, Texas Long Horn bulls, and five imported head of purebred Angus. Eli, as a banker and part owner, managed to procure two government contracts three years later. He then came out to join his nephew Rance, in running the ranch; thus, the name GL7 Ranch was founded.

Tim, had gone back east to an Illinois financial law and business school, and now, he took care of all the finances, buying and selling business of the ranch. Tim's older brother, James was in charge of all the upkeep of the ranch and property. Vern, who was no doubt some relative, Tim hadn't mentioned, as of yet, was the ranch foreman, in charge of about twenty or thirty ranch hands, and all the care and keep of their large herd of cattle and horses. Tim's mother, was in the house with the housemaid, Mei-Li, preparing food for the gathering.

Eli Gustafson, had move out West with his wife and his niece, Rance Logan's sister, Tim's aunt. Eli's wife had died just two years earlier of pneumonia, and his niece still lived with him and took care of the aging Gustafson. Tim told us, Eli was a hardnosed old bird, who loved the open range for cattle and hated fences; he, also hated sheep because, he said, they eat off the grass too close to the ground, ruining it for cattle and horses.

Eli had his house, a little more than a mile away, and, there was a large bunk house, where all, but a few of the hired hands stayed. I wasn't sure, but it seemed that Tim Logan, didn't share his great uncles feelings on open range and sheep, however, he kept his thoughts pretty well to himself.

While we were talking with Tim, about a dozen or so cowboys drifted in and joined the two out at the spit, which now, had burned down to an inferno of red hot coals, ready to hang the side of beef. As a few of the cowboys, out by the spit, lifted the side of beef and hug it over the fire, five riders came into the lot; two broke off and joined the others out at the spit, while three, continue up toward the house.

"Good, they're here," said Tim as he stood up and stepped off the porch to meet them. "Come on fellas, I want you to meet some of my family. Kid Carrey, I especially want you to meet, Vern. Vern, is quite a gun hand too."

"Fancy that," said George curiously.

I took note of the three riders as they approached; there was an older, grey at the temples, yet sturdy looking man, I figured, must be Tim's father, Rance Logan. Then, there was a man that looked like a younger version of him, I was pretty sure that was James, Tim's brother. The last rider, who no doubt was Vern, was tall, slim and sat unusually straight in the saddle, for a cowhand. This rider, wore tan canvass pants, an off white, dust soiled shirt and a long, dark brown, leather vest, and was topped off, with a grey, sweat stained, wide brimmed pan-cake hat, held on by a leather chin strap. There just seemed to be something odd about this last rider, I just couldn't put a finger on it. They all got off their horses at the same time and tied them off. I noticed a .45 Schofield, with a polished, bone handle, holstered low on the front hip of the tall rider. I figured, this must be Vern.

As they stepped toward us, Tim started the introductions. First, he introduced the greying man as his father, Rance Logan; just as I had thought. Next, the younger rider, as his brother James; they both greeted us friendly like, with a firm hand shake. "And now," said Tim, "I want you to meet, Vern."

I extended my hand, as Vern loosened the chin strap and pushed up the hat and let it fall back to the end of the chin strap. It was then, I notice the bright, piercing, blue eyes, as thick, long, wavy, blond hair tumbled down around Vern's shoulders.

"Vern's a woman?" I said dumbfounded, as she shook her hair out. A woman indeed; Vern was a mature woman, with strong features, yet she was shapely and very attractive.

"Yep," Tim said, with a laugh. "Meet my Aunt, Veronica."

She shook my hand as firm as the others had, smiled and said, "Most, just call me Vern, for short.

Veronica, is kind'a long winded, out here in the West."

Then, she turned to George and extended a hand, saying, "And, you must be Kid Carrey, the man that killed, Mean Gene Green, before, I had cause too. Thanks, for saving my nephews butt. I'm, kind'a fond of'm." Rance and James nodded in agreement.

George paused, with his head cocked slightly, for a long moment; he seemed reluctant to shake hands with Vern. I wasn't sure why. Finally, he smiled and raised his hand and said, "So, you wanted to meet me? I here yer pretty handy with that Schofield."

"Well, I suppose I am," said Vern. "You don't mince words, do ya? Maybe later, we can have a little friendly competition; just for fun of course."

"Just for fun, of course," repeated George. "I'm anxious to see what ya have in mind."

George's lips tightened and his eyes narrowed. The two of them, glared into one another's eyes, until a buckboard came rumbling noisily across the lot, with a family of five onboard, and interrupted the moment.

Tim said, "Wel-l now, that that's over, let's go out and meet some other folks we invited."

As we walked out to where the spit was, a carriage, a wagon and three riders on horseback arrived to join the party.

Tim introduced us to most of the people that were there and those that came in a little later. We met many of the cowhands, that worked the ranch, most seemed quite, reserved and kept to themselves. We also, met a few of the neighbor ranchers, their families and then, the County Deputy Sheriff and his family. The one person, we didn't met, that we thought we would, was Eli Gustafson. We found out from someone, that because of an incurable illness, Eli didn't venture out much, but still was pretty much in charge, of GL7 Cattle Company Ranch.

Tim's mother and the Asian house servant, brought out large dishes of prepared vegetables and buttered potatoes, not to mention a number of cakes and pies. George, pretty well made a pig of himself, when it came to the fresh baked apple pie, his real favorite, by the way.

After everyone seemed to have finished eating and were milling around talking, Vern got everyone's attention, calling, "Hey ya'll, gather round and follow me, we're gonna have us a little shootin' contest. Come on, Kid Carrey, let's have some fun."

"Lead the way, pretty lady," said George, as he bowed and gestured with his hand, for her to go on ahead.

"It's, damned seldom, anyone calls me a lady," Vern said.

"I call'm, like I see'm," replied George.

Vern smirked a laugh, and proceeded to lead the crowd around the barn, where there was a couple cords of fire wood, stacked up, about twenty feet away from the back of the barn. She gave instructions to one of the ranch hands who, though being dark skinned, didn't seem to be of Mexican descent. He had long, black, greying hair, that ran from under a narrow brimmed sombrero, down his back to his shoulder blades; he had a dark, thin mustache that blended into neatly trimmed chin whiskers. The man was clothed in a dark brown, baroque stitched shirt, a vest, chinos and a holster outfit, that was all accented with silver Conchos and leather lacing, which held a Pearl griped, Remington .44, conversion six-shooter. "Pecos," she said, "get a dozen or so, tin cans out of the barrel and bend the lids off. Set the cans on top the wood pile and get some horseshoe nails, and drive them into the center of the lids and nail them to the end of some of the logs out there."

Pecos just nodded, and went about doing, what he was told to do. Meanwhile, Vern distanced herself, about twenty-five paces away from the wood pile, and started explaining how this was going to work. "We'll, see who's the fastest by which can flies off the wood pile first. Then, we'll see who's aim is the sharpest. You see, those can lids won't fall off, unless, your bullet drives that nail square into the wood.

"Anyone else want to join in the competition?" asked Vern.

Pecos responded immediately, "Yeah," he called.

The Deputy Sheriff said, "It might be interesting, just for fun." Those two, were the only others takers.

After Pecos rejoined the group, Vern started explaining how this was going to play out. "Pecos, you take the first can on the left," she said. "Deputy, the next one. Kid Carrey, how about you shoot at the last can on the right and, I'll take the one next to it. What we'll do, is have Tim, count to five, and we'll all draw and shoot, and the crowd can decide, who's can flies off first; fair enough?" Everyone agreed, and Vern said, "Y'all ready? Okay Tim, give us a five count."

Tim counted, "One- Two- Three- Four— Five." **BOOM-BOOM-BOOM—BOOM** Four blast, in rapid sequence, sent three of the cans flying off the wood pile; the Deputy missed. To my disbelief, Vern had beat George by a measure, and Pecos, came in a very close third. Not only did the Sheriff, miss his mark, but he was notably, slow on the draw. Fortunately, a good lawman doesn't have to be the best gun hand around, to be effective at his job.

As the crowd made their judgment, Vern smiled, self-satisfied; she had beat George. George, he didn't seem a bit bothered about the outcome. Pecos, had a definite scowl of disappointment on his face. The Deputy, just shrugged and chuckled, as he shook his head.

"Not bad, boys," said Vern. "Now, let's see who can hit where they look. We'll see how many can lids we can drop with three shots. Pecos, you first."

"I'ight," he said, and then, he took careful aim and fired; one can lid fell. It took two shots to get the next one to fall.

"Sheriff, you're next," said Vern. The Sheriff nodded and took his time. Two times, he aimed and fired but, it took three shots for one lid to fall.

Vern smiled at George, and said, "Alright, Kid Carrey, see what you can do."

"No-No," said George. "Ladies first, I insist."

"Lady my ass." Vern puckered her brow and gave half a smile. "But— alright. I'll shoot first," she said, "Since, you insist."

Vern took dead on aim, and BANG, one lid fell. And again, BANG, a second lid fell, and BANG; the third lid had a bullet hole taking a fraction from the nail head, but leaving the lid hanging.

All the other shooters had taken careful aim when they fired. Four lids, counting the one Vern left hanging remained. George's .45s were both holstered at his sides and no sooner had Vern finished shooting when, George drew both pistols and dropped the four lids and then shot the two remaining cans on top of the wood pile. Then, he spun the pistols in his hands and planted the firmly back in place. The crowd was speechless. Vern's jaw tightened, and her eyes narrowed at this action as she glared at George.

George snickered, "Oops— Sorry," he said. "I guess, I got a little carried away there."

"Go to hell, Carrey," Vern said, "Good shootin' though, even if ya ain't so fast."

"O-h, it'll get me by," said George.

"You know," said Vern, "we could use another decent gun-hand around here; if, you're in need of employment Carrey, and of course we could use you too Cash?"

"Me? No," said George. "I'm a gambling man. Don't believe in gettin' dirty, or, nosin' around in fusses over dumb animals. Besides, it might conflict with Cash's new job with Mister Martinez and John Grey-Wolf."

Pecos's blue eyes burned, icy cold, and he butted in, "Folks around here, don't take ta stinkin', sheep-men. Besides, I hear ther kind'a prone to fallin' off ther hosses, over cliffs."

"Would you have some firsthand knowledge about that, would you, Pecos?" asked George.

Pecos smiled, "Naw, just heard the rumor, ther clumsy," he said. "A man could come to harm hangin' round with 'em sheep-men."

"Sounds like a threat," I said and I stepped toward Pecos.

"Not no threat," said Pecos as he stepped forward matching my move. "It's shore the hell, a damned shore fact a nature though."

Vern, moved between Pecos and me, saying as she stood nose to nose with him, "Alright fellas, we don't need any blood here today. This is a friendly, get together."

"I don't get friendly, with no stinkin', sheep man," said Pecos. "Just as soon shoot 'em, as look at 'em."

"Back off, and shut-up, Pecos," said Vern.

"Shore, Boss. At least fer now; but, this ain't gonna be the end of this, if, yer stupid enough to tie in with the likes of Martinez an' Johnny Grey-Wolf." said Pecos. Then, he stepped back and calmed himself a bit.

Vern, tightened her lips, and narrowed her brow. "That's quite enough, Pecos," she said. She looked at George. "You know, I kind'a like you fellas. And, I do, appreciate what you did helping my nephew and all; but, sheep-herdin' around here is a dangerous profession. Could, even be deadly."

George, moved in close with Vern; his serious, expression focused in on hers. "Let me make something, real clear, right here, and now. If anything, was to happen to Cash, not that he can't take care of himself, I would take it personal and would not hesitate, to put a bullet between the eyes of anyone who would cause him any kind of harm, at any time. Understood?"

"Ain't, a'feared a you, Carrey," said Pecos.

"Good. Maybe, then, to save some time and trouble later, you and me could do the deal right now, Pecos?" said George.

Before he had a chance to respond, "PECOS: dammit," Vern interrupted, "Go spend some time with the rest of the hands. NOW, Pecos," she ordered.

"Yeah Boss, shore. It's gonna happen, Carrey," said Pecos, as he turned and headed toward where the others were by the fire. " It's gonna happen."

"You, bet'cha," George said.

"Like I said," repeated Vern, "I like you fellas. I wouldn't want to see any grief come to either of you."

"We're not the ones should be worryin' about any grief," said George. "Cash and me can pretty well take care of our own business. Maybe yer bunch, ought to do the same."

"As long as your business don't interfere with ours, we'll do that," Vern said. "But we're not gonna tolerate fencing open range and the ruining good grass land."

Tim who had kept quiet through all of this, now spoke up saying, "These men are my guests and I think it's time to drop this conversation, and, show the proper hospitality."

"Tim, you know how we all feel about sheep ranchers and the trouble they cause," said Rance Logan. "This is cattle country boys, and they need to understand that, and take their sheep herds somewhere else."

"We could all work it out somehow, and make room for everybody," said Tim, "That is, if you and Eli weren't so damned stubborn and used some common sense."

"You need to hold your tongue son; remember who you are," said Rance Logan. "This ain't for debate. That's the way it is and it's not going to get any better until those sheep herders move out."

"I don't know, Pop," said James, joining the conversation, "Maybe, Tim has a point."

"We ain't discussin' this anymore," said Rance and he turned and stomped off.

"Sorry Tim," I said, "It's about time we leave, huh George?"

"Yeah Cash, I think we've worn out our welcome. Best idea, I've heard today," said George.

Tim frowned and looked down at the ground and said, "Sorry, not the way I intended things to go."

"Well, I hate to see you fellas leave in an unfriendly spirit," Vern said. "If y'all stay on the right side of this deal, we'll all come out fine."

"Well," I said, "I'm sure you're gonna do what you're gonna do, and I'm gonna do the same."

"Best take mind of what I said," Vern warned.

"Best take mind of what I said," replied George. "Remind Pecos, I'm a man of my word to a fault." With that George and me headed for our horses and mounted up to leave. Pecos, and the bunch he was standing with, gave us a hard, threatening, stare as we rode by.

Cash and Carrey

## X

Other than a glance or two, there was no conversation between George and me, until we were well past the entrance gate of the GL7 ranch. I spoke up first, "Ya reckon," I asked, " we should have mentioned my working for Martinez and Grey-Wolf?"

"We-ll," said George, "I figured we'd might as well lay our cards on the table and let them know where we stood. And, I think we pretty well got the gist of their way of thinkin' on it."

"I suppose we did all that, and more," I said. "I see trouble comin' from that Pecos fella. Don't trust he'll be upfront about it neither; maybe, a back shootin' skunk, I'm a thinkin'."

"I'd say, there's a good chance you're right about that, Cash," said George. "And, you know, I feel kind'a the same way about ol' Vern as well."

"Yep, not too far off on that one either," I said.

When we got back in town, I went straight to the hotel to get some rest. George went and helped Lydia close the restaurant; after that, he found an all-night poker game at one of the saloons.

Sunday, after breakfast at the Price House Restaurant, of course, George and me spent the day wondering around, looking the place over and getting familiar with the town and some of the people. A number of folks recognized George as Kid Carrey, the one who shot, Mean Gene Green.

Most expressed gratitude, for getting rid of a no-count, murdering, trouble maker.

Me, George, Lydia and her son Eric, went just outside of town by the cemetery, in a little clearing under some trees, and had a basket dinner of fried chicken. George and Lydia took a long walk, while Eric and me skipped rocks across a little pond that was nearby. I wasn't sure, but I was beginning to think that George might be considering settling down there.

Monday morning, found me at the Martinez place, ready to learn something about droving sheep.

For the next couple of months we herded sheep, with the help of three outstandingly trained and dedicated dogs, from one patch of range grass to the next. We kept an eye out for wolves and coyote that might attack the herd. We also mended fence, almost every day, that had been pulled down and broken. At night, one or two of us, would watch over the herd. I worked with Mr. Martinez, his oldest son Hector, and Ira, John Grey-Wolf's nephew. Once a week or so, Martinez's daughter Antoinette or John Grey-Wolf, in a hay wagon, would come and work with us for a day.

In the meantime, George would be found at either the Price Restaurant, or playing poker most of the night, at one of the saloons in town.

The weather was turning grey and cold in the mountains; the necessity to mend fence had lessened to maybe, once a week. There was still grass, but it was brown now, as was most all plant growth in the surrounding hills.

Martinez told me, that in a few more weeks, we would be securing the herd in pins up by the houses for the winter, and feed hay and grain.

One particular cold afternoon, as icy snow crystals blew sideways, and, Mr. Martinez and I sat wrapped in blankets, trying to keep warm by the camp fire, George rode up and informed us that, Eli Gustafson had died in his sleep, and that there would be a graveside funeral service in a couple days, on Saturday. George suggested, that him and me attend, for the benefit of Tim and Vern, and to see if any attitudes had changed due to Eli's passing. Mr. Martinez said, 'he thought that would be a respectful thing to do,'; so, I agreed to join him'.

The day of the funeral, I met George at the Price House Restaurant at about seven in the morning. The funeral was scheduled to start at ten; George and me had a chance to catch up on our plans for moving on. Our money situation was just a few dollars shy of $4,000 in our poke. It seemed things had leveled off between, the GL7 Ranch and the Martinez, Gray-Wolf outfits; there hadn't been any damaged fence, or bad talk in nearly a month. It seemed, after talking awhile, that any plans George was making for the future, was probably going to include Lydia and her son. I had no idea, how drastically, things were about to change. George, and I decided to put off making any definite plan until Spring, since, it was pretty peaceful right now.

George and me sat sipping coffee and talking for quite a spell, then we noticed the procession moving down the street toward the cemetery. Rance and Vern, were in the lead on horseback, close behind them was a fancy, polished, brass trimmed, black hearse, with full view, side windows. So, the first, last, and only glimpse, of Eli Gustafson we got was a pale, lifeless body, in a black suit, in an open casket, carried in the back of that hearse. Following the hearse, there were about thirty to forty people; most on foot, a few on horseback and a couple carriages. George and me, went outside, as we had decided, to take up the rear behind everyone else.

Slowly, the procession made its way up to the cemetery. Once inside, the crowd made a half circle around a large polished, ornate, granite, grave marker; there were two names on it. One name was, Maureen Veronica Gustafson, and the other was for, Eliezer Rance Gustafson.

Vern, Rance, James and Tim, stood, shoulder to shoulder together, beside the grave. Vern's hair was tied back, she was dressed in a black skirt and jacket, wearing a white laced blouse. A very striking woman, to look at. She wasn't totally, out of character though; she had her Schofield .45 hanging heavy on her hip under the jacket.

A tall, thin fellow, in a long black coat and a straight brimmed, black hat, went to the head of the grave, by the marker. He removed his hat and stood looking down, while, four pallbearers, closed the lid to the casket and carried it to the open grave and sat it down on two planks, laying across the hole. Everyone, had their attention focused on the fellow at the head of the grave, and he began to speak; just as he did, Rance, looked up and saw us on the other side of the grave. He elbowed Vern, and nodded toward us. She looked over at us, and her brow narrowed; flames of rage, filled her piercing blue eyes. She held her hand up to the tall man, in the black coat. She ordered, "HOLD—it a damned minute, preacher man."

Everyone was wide eyed and quiet, as Vern sternly marched around the casket, to where we were. She stopped, standing eye to eye with George, and said, "Kid Carrey, I appreciate you bein' here, out of respect for my family, I'm sure. But, this," she glared at me, with intense distain, "stinkin', sheepman, is certainly not welcome, and if he doesn't get out of my sight, pronto, I'm gonna put a bullet in his forehead."

I started to take a step forward, but George moved between us. I never saw him look so mean and unpleasant. "Cash is my kin," he said, "and, I don't take kindly, to anyone's insulting words, toward him. And, make no mistake about it, Cash, might go down in a fight, but, I assure you, he'll take some with him. Let me tell you all, here today; I would kill anybody, man, or women, that ever brought any harm to him in anyway, anytime. If he, is not welcome, nor am I. Out of respect for this grievous time for your family, we'll be leavin'. But, if bullets are gonna fly, I'd be happy to oblige ya any other time." George looked at me, smiled large, and said, "Let's go get some pie, Cash."

Pecos, who had been standing with a small group of other GL7 cowhands, stepped out, and barked, "Yer gonna get yers, sheepman."

"That's right," said Vern, as we started to leave.

I turned and smiled, "Bring 'er on lady."

## XI

Martinez, was talking seriously about rounding up the herd and driving them up to the pins at the end of October, but, then the weather cleared and became unseasonably warm. So, Grey-Wolf and Martinez decided, to postpone the round-up, for a little while.

I took a couple days off, and went into town the second Saturday, in November, and found George, helping out at the restaurant. With further inquiry, I found out that, Lydia had become very ill, with a high fever. The town doctor, was treating her for pneumonia, but didn't seem to be having much success, in controlling her temperature. George, was either at her bedside, or, helping in the restaurant; he never left. After, talking with George that night, I realized, I had never seen him so troubled about anything. There, was surely, no doubt about George's feelings, about Lydia.

I stayed the night, in George's hotel room in town, since, I wasn't expected back at the Grey-Wolf, Martinez's outfit, until Monday, late afternoon. I had, brought the wagon in to get some supplies. George hardly slept, because, of Lydia's delirious moaning's, all night long. Everyone, was expecting her fever to break at any time; they kept cold towels on her constantly. However, it wasn't to be; Lydia passed early, Sunday morning, just before daybreak.

I had never, seen George shed a tear, ever. Even when we were kids, he would get hurt and maybe curse, but, never cry. However, that day, he wept silently for hours, as he sat with Lydia's son, Eric and Momma Price, after she had passed. Then George, me, and the Doctor moved her to the undertakers office, to have him prepare her for burial.

For the rest of the day, George, wasn't fit company for no one; he didn't have a kind word in any of the small amount of conversation, he had. Finally, in the early afternoon, he went to the saloons, to drink and gamble. Price's Restaurant, was closed of course, and I spent the day talking to Momma Price, about her plans for the future. She decided, that after a memorial service, to be held at the restaurant, she was going to put Price's Restaurant up for sale, and move her and Eric, back East, since she no longer had anything, worthwhile in Springerville.

Around, eight o'clock that evening, I decided, I'd better check on George. I found him in one of the saloons in town, drinking heavy and losing money. That wasn't normal for him, for he usually, drank little, and called it in, when the cards weren't running right. I stepped up to the bar and ordered two fingers, of rye, and watched, as George mostly lost, every hand. Finally, I had enough of watching this, so, after downing another two fingers, I went over to the table where he and three other rugged looking hombre's, were playing Draw Poker.

I stood to George's side, and said while one of the other men was dealing, "Say George, what do ya say, we call it a night. It's been a pretty rough day, and, I think, we're both in need of some rest."

The cowboy that had just dealt the hand, was setting across the table from George, he said, "Hey, jack-ass, can't ya see, we're playin' cards here. So, why don't ya butt out, an' get lost."

"Why, don't you mind your own business, mister," I responded.

"W-ell, I'll put a big hole in yer face, boy," he answered.

I returned sharply, "Stand up, and go to work there, Cowboy."

The big fellas dark eyes narrowed in response as he stood and kicked his chair, hard, behind him, sending it tumbling across the floor.

By the time the fella was upright, with his hand to a Star .44 that was, stuffed in the front of his pants; George, had his right hand Colt pointed, dead in the center of the man's chest, and, I had drawn my .45, cocked, and ready to fire.

"Unless, you wanna be the one dyin', don't be talkin' to my cousin like that, or, you'll deal with me," said George, as he pushed his hat back on his head, with his pistol barrel.

"S-h-o-r-e, Kid. Honest, I dent know he's yer kin. Sor'y, 'bout that, mister," the big man said. He went after his chair. "Truly, am sor'y, Kid," he said as he carefully sat back down at the table.

"Now Cash, why, don't you mind yer own business," said George, as he holstered his six-gun. "If ya need some rest, go on over to the hotel room," he said stoutly, as he tossed a five dollar chip into the pot.

"You sure are losing a lot of our money, George," I said.

"Hey, you do the sheep herdin', an' I'll do the gamblin', okay Cash," said George.

"All right then, George. Have it your way, ya damned grouch." I turned and left before I lost my temper, realizing, George wasn't himself, because of the loss of Lydia.

So, I did just what George suggested, I headed for the hotel. I figured, that George would give it up soon, I just didn't know, how much of our poke would be gone, before he did.

## XII

I was sleeping pretty sound, when about half-past midnight, I was awakened suddenly, by gun shots down in the street. I jumped into my britches and stumbled to the window, to take a look at what was going on.

As I focused on a figure down in the middle of the street, I realized, it was George; he was reloading his .45's. When, he got both pistols loaded, he commenced firing into the air, as if, he were shooting at something up above him. I strained at the window to look up at what he was aiming at. George cussed, as he stumbled and weaved along, to keep his balance. He would stretch out his arms, firing each pistol, one at a time, at the unseen target. Finally, with my cheek pressed against the cool glass, I looked up, and realized, he was shooting at an almost full, bright moon, that lit up the night.

I quickly pulled on my britches and slipped into my boots and shirt; then, I headed down the stairs to where George was outside, in the street. As I got there, George, was dry firing his pistols and got ready to reload again.

"George, ol' pard," I called, "Don't shoot me. But, what are you doing?"

He looked over at me, and slowly collapsed to his knees with his pistol hanging down at his sides in his hands. "Why…Cash? Why'd, she have to die," George sobbed. "I loved her so much, Cash. She meant everything to me, and now she's gone. Dam-it, WHY?"

"Don't know cousin. I just don't know," I said, as I helped him to his feet. "Let's get out of the street and go get some rest, Pard."

"Okay, Cash," he replied. "I'm so'ry fer earlier, Cash. I'm, just so damned mad, and, I don't understand."

"Not a problem here, ol' buddy. I understand, I wish I had an answer, but I don't."

A cool breeze was starting to stir up some crystal flakes of snow, as clouds moved in and overwhelmed the target moon, George had been shooting at. I couldn't help but think as we headed toward the hotel, of how necessary it was to bring the sheep herd in for the winter. Martinez and Grey-Wolf, would need all the help they could get to accomplish it.

Next morning, George and I had a long talk about what our plans were now. I had figured he had lost a lot of our money in the poker game the night before, however he informed me he actually ended up winning a little over fifty dollars.

George wanted to pack up and leave right after the memorial service on Friday afternoon at the restaurant. Mrs. Price had decided, she was taking Lydia's body back east, to be buried in the family grave site.

I explained to George, the need for me to stay, long enough to help the ranch move the sheep herds in for the winter, after that there wouldn't be much for me to do out there anyway. George understood, and that is what we planned around; we would leave after the herd was all settled in. I would be back in town for the memorial service and go back out to the ranch if needed.

We spent the rest of the day together having a few beers and gathering possibles for moving on, when the time came. We turned in early that night, so, I could get back out to the ranch early the next morning.

Martinez and Grey-Wolf were glad to see me; they had already moved a third of the herd up from the range, and were getting ready to head back out.

Martinez ask if, I was ready to go out with them. I said, "Shore, that's what I am here for."

John Grey-Wolf was setting in the seat of a buckboard, and his wheelchair, was secured in the back. It took most of the day to get out on the range and round up the rest of the sheep. Hector and Grey-Wolf's daughter, Nitara, had spent the night with the heard and now they and Martinez were going to drive half of what was there back to the pens; they would get the pens ready for the next bunch, that me and Grey-Wolf, would bring in the next morning.

Grey-Wolf and I made camp in a group of pines on the top of an overhang, that dropped off sharply, to about sixty or seventy feet above a rocky, dried up river bed. We built our fire about ten to fifteen yards from the edge of the precipice. John and I had become better acquainted over the time I had been there, and, he realized, I was upholding my part of the deal.

We kept watch in two hour shifts while maintaining the fire. I left John in front of the fire, in his wheelchair, with his rifle across his lap, after I had finished third watch.

I was jolted awake by John's yelling; somehow, Pecos, had got the drop on Grey-Wolf and was pushing him at a run toward the edge of the overhang. "Can you fly ijun?" he laughed as he ran along. I stood up quick as I could, and reached for my pistol, however, before I could clear leather someone mounted behind me dropped a lasso over me and pulled me off my feet and through the fire. I heard Grey-Wolf holler, as he was dumped over the cliff, out of his wheelchair. There was no chance this time of him surviving the fall on the rocks below.

I was bounced and dragged along, over sage brush, rocks and an occasional paddle cactus for quite a spell; nearly knocked out a number of times, before it finally ended. I twisted myself over and saw who the mounted rider was in the moon light, it was Vern. About that time, Pecos held up beside her, quickly dismounted and came over to me; he gave me a hard kick in the ribs and started to give me another, when Vern called him off, thankfully.

"I think this sheep man and Kid Carrey will see we mean business now. Cash, I would have let Pecos finish you off, if you fellas hadn't saved my nephew. So, you and Carrey ride on out of this and no more will be said. If you don't leave, you'll both be dead the next time."

It was cold and spitting snow, the icy flakes blowing in my face were bringing me back to focus. It was then, I realized my hand was on my .45, my mind imagined Grey-Wolf going over that precipice, so, without giving it a second thought, I drew my Colt and fired a shot square into Pecos' chest. The last thing I remember after that, was hearing Vern's Schofield speak loud and painful.

My eyes flickered open in the light as I awoke. I wasn't sure if I was alive or not. As my head started to clear, things came into view, I realized I was in the back room of the doctor's office, laying on the operating table. George, Martinez and the Deputy Sheriff, were there waiting for me to come round.

I tried to lift myself up, but it was pointless, I could hardly move, my ribs and left shoulder were bandaged heavily. I started to talk, but it came out, not much more than a whisper. "Vern, Pecos…And, John?"

George came over to me, "Don't try to talk Cash. We know the whole story. Vern, brought you into Martinez, on the back of Pecos' horse. She dumped you and told him, Pecos shoved Grey-Wolf off a cliff, he's dead. She said, you shot Pecos and she shot you after dragging you a while. She told Martinez, to clear out of the Valley or he and his family, would be the next to die and be burned out. She said that, she and her family would be in town for the memorial service Friday, and unless we rode out right after, there would be a show down."

I grabbed George's shirt in my fist, "You can't go up against her," I whispered. "She's, faster than you."

"I don't think so, Cash. I was testin' them out to see what they had that day. No way, is she faster'n me," he assured. "An', there's no way, I'll let her get away with this. You just rest easy, and heel up. It'll be alright."

"I don't think ya ought to be havin' no gun fight with a woman, 'specially with Vern. That family's friends of mine," said the Deputy.

"I made it clear what would happen should anyone, bring harm to Cash," said George. "Since it don't seem like you wanna deal with these people for their criminality, then I most certainly will."

"Al'm the law 'round here, and, I decide who the criminals are. I ain't takin' the word of no sheep man on this deal quite yet. I mean, your pard killed a man and, how do I know whether it was in self-defense or not. You cause trouble for that family and you'll find yerself behind bars or at the end of a rope. That's the way I see it."

"Sounds to me," said George, "you might just be on the wrong side of that badge, like some other fellows, I know. And, though I do respect the law, you get in my way, and, you just might pay the dealer."

"Don'cha threaten me ya two bit gambler. Ya might be able to take me in a straight up gunfight, but I'll deputize more'n half this town and bring'm down on ya, if I need to, an' you'll be the one payin'."

"Maybe so, Deputy," George said, "but you'll be the first one I'll be aimin' at. Keep that in mind when ya come, Deputy."

"Al'm a thinkin,' you'd do good to take Vern's advice, and move on outta here while yer still upright," said the Deputy as he walked out and slammed the door behind him.

Martinez came over to me and George and started apologizing for getting us involve in this trouble. "With John murdered, and you hurt, sẽnior Cash, maybe…maybe, I will be selling out and moving my family also," he said.

"It's not right, that hard workin' folks, like yourselves, should be run off by a bunch of no count cowpuncher's," George said; I was not expecting that out of him.

"Well, now…now, that John is gone and with sẽnior Cash hurt and in a bad way; I have had all I can stomach. Not only that, I have to do what is best for my family."

"Suite yourself, but these people ain't gonna get away with what they've done. I can assure you of that," George said.

"George," I said, as I tightened my grip on his shirt, "If Mr. Martinez is gonna give it up, then, I think we should too."

"W-ell, Cash," said George, "I didn't start this ruckus, but I can sure the hell finish it. I ain't gonna let anyone get away with this, man nor woman."

About that time, the Doctor came in room and walked over to where I was laying. "You need rest, young man," said the Doctor. "Here," he instructed, "you fellas, help me get him off this table, and on to the cot in the other room."

Once they got me comfortable, the Doctor told everyone, that it would be a couple of days before I would be able to get around on my own; then, I would still need to take it easy for at least a month.

On Thursday morning, I was able to walk, with a little help from George, to the hotel. Other than eating meals, George brought to me that Mrs. Price prepared, I pretty well stayed in bed resting; I didn't want to miss the memorial service for Lydia on Friday. George, stayed around the hotel most of the time, we played penny-ante poker to pass the time. George, of course, won most of the time; he beat me out of about three dollars, altogether.

## XIII

On Friday, we were up early, and having breakfast down at the restaurant. Mama Price had fixed a fine meal of eggs, bacon and fresh biscuits. The Memorial Service at the restaurant, was to be at two in the afternoon, a local traveling preacher was to preside. After breakfast, I took my time walking back to the hotel to rest up, while George, helped Mrs. Price clean up the place.

George and me, arrived at the restaurant, a little after one. People started coming in about one thirty or so. I think more than half the town was there. About ten minutes to the hour, Vern, Rance and Tim, came through the door. When, George spotted Vern, his eyes glassed with angry. He was not wearing his pistol outfit, in respect for the service; he had hung them up in the kitchen. Apparently, Vern and Rance, had no such state of mind. They, were the only persons indiscreetly, toting six-guns. George, without hesitation, marched right up and blocked their path.

"What the hell makes you think, yer welcome here, Vern?" asked George, "I mean…Tim, you can stay. You two, best clear out, now."

With a cock-eyed smile, Vern replied, "Pretty strong talk, for a man that ain't heeled."

"You, really wanna push this, here and now?" asked George, "Or, are you the cold hearted varmint, I think you are?"

Vern put her hand to the Schofield at her side, Tim grabbed her hand and held it down, "No. Not here...not now," he insisted, "Let's just leave."

"Alright Tim, just for you this time," Vern said. "But, when this breaks up and the crowd clears; I'll meet you out in the street, Carrey."

"If yer shore, that's what you wanna do, then, I'll be happy to oblige ya," said George.

"Now, is this gonna be me and you, or do I need to face all three of ya?"

Tim said, "Wait a minute, I want no part in this play."

"I'm sure," said Vern, with the same cock-eyed smirk on her face, "I am all you won't, be able to handle, Kid."

"Well," said George, "I'm looking forward to it. But, just to let you know and ta be fair, I held back a bit out at the ranch that day."

"Kid Carrey, I will beat you on yer best day, hands down," promised Vern.

"It'll be interestin' fer shore. I've never killed a woman before."

"Don't let that slow ya down. I'm aimin' to take yer head off, Kid," Vern declared.

"Just remember what I said would happen if any harm came to Cash. I don't blow wind about that."

"Ya don't rattle me none. You just be out in the street; don't make me come and get ya."

"I wouldn't miss it for the world, Lady," said George.

"You'll soon find out who's a damned lady, you son-a-bitch."

George's anger blazed white hot; that just wasn't something you called him, ever. In an instant he back handed Vern across the mouth.

Vern hardly flinched; she turned her head and spit blood to the side. Rance started to make a move, but Vern held him back with her arm. She smiled through bloody teeth and said, "We'll soon have this settled buck·o."

"Ya bet we will. Nobody, causes Cash harm or calls me that and doesn't pay the price," George said.

"See you in the street Carrey."

She elbowed Rance, and nodded toward the door. The three turned and left; I had kept quite through the whole thing. George came over to me and I said, "Damn George, you shore pushed that to the edge, didn't ya?"

"Yeah, 'fraid so. And, I can't believe I'm gonna kill a woman today. I'd have never thought, but if a woman ever needed killin', that one does."

"I don't know George, just a little different game you're playin' here. Don't take that wrong though, I got yer back cuz."

"Yeah, you and me, just like always. I appreciate that, thanks Cash."

Mrs. Price came over, "We're ready to start boys." So we took our seats.

The local traveling preacher spoke for a while and then people came up one at a time to testify about their personal experiences and relationship with Lydia. After about a dozen or so people spoke and sat back down, then to my surprise, George got up and said something. "I think ya'all know what my feelings were toward Lydia. I loved her, she was the nicest woman I have ever known outside of my Aunt DeWhite, who raised me and Cash. I'll miss her ter'ibly; I won't ever feel that strong about another woman as long as I live." Then George sat down.

The Preacher man lead the crowd in singing a hymn, then Mom Price thanked everyone for coming and they started given their condolences as they slowly filed out.

George spoke some kind words to Mrs. Price and then started strapping on his two pistol outfit. That is when I remembered I had left my firearms at the hotel.

I went to Mrs. Price and asked, "Is there any guns in the restaurant?"

"No, I…" she paused. "Maybe in the back of the pantry. My son kept a shotgun of some kind there."

"Thanks Mrs. Price. Do you mind if I look?"

"No sure, go ahead. I know nothing about guns anyway."

I went to the kitchen pantry and searched for the shotgun. I spotted it tucked away, leaning in a back corner. I pulled it out and broke it open; it was a Wm. Moore & Co. coach-gun, loaded with 10 gauge buckshot. I looked all around and could not find any more shells for it. As I started to step out of the pantry I saw one lone shell, standing up, next to a coal oil lamp on a shelf. I thought, 'Three shells with a close range shot-gun, guess it's better than nothing.'

When I came out of the kitchen, George was by the front door looking out of the window to see what the situation was outside. I went over and stood beside him. "George," I asked, "you really wanna kill a woman?"

"Well, no. Don't see where I've got much choice though."

"What's it look like out there?" I asked.

"Vern's over on the other side of the street there," George pointed with his chin, "by the water trough, checkin' the action and playing with the Schofield. Rance is a few yards up the boardwalk from her with his Winchester. And, I think there's a ranch hand this side of the street tucked between here and the building next door."

"I can sure 'nough take care of the fellow on this side of the street, but, I don't see how I can do that and get to Rance, before he lets go with that rifle. I'll save a barrel for him if I can."

"Well Cash, I'll keep him between me and Vern a few feet when I move on her. I'll use my right hand for her, and save my left for when Rance makes his move. If you move in on him, be close, I don't want you to hit me with any of that scattergun buckshot.

"Well, ya ready Cash?"

"Let's do it, George."

George opened the door and Mrs. Pierce said, "Take care, boys." George gave her a nod and lead the way through the door. When outside, George stepped into the street and slowly walked in Vern's direction; a few paces before aligning himself to the left with Rance, he stopped, so as to keep him in full sight. Vern, holstered the Schofield and moved to middle of the street keeping her hand on the pistol.

Me, after I stepped through the doorway, I eased my why down the side of the building toward the ranch hand in the narrow alleyway between the buildings. I could only see, about a third of the man's front side, standing there. He did not see me, because his attention, was focused on the street. I moved on down, as close as I dared, without being noticed. I froze in place like a hunting dog on point, then I rested the shotgun on my slung forearm and eased the double hammers silently back.

Vern took a firm stance and loosened her shoulders, George did the same.

"We-l-l now," said Vern, "Here we are. I think we both knew that it would come down to this."

"Yeah maybe," George said. "Ya know, I ain't really hankerin' to shoot a woman. What say, me and Cash leave town today and just call it a draw?"

"Don't go yella on me now, Carrey."

"I'm shore you know better'n that Vern."

"Then, go fer yer ir'ns Kid."

"Naw," George smiled, "you know how it is."

Vern's eyes narrowed and she raised a questioning eyebrow. "What?"

George gave her a wink and said, "Ladies first."

Vern's blue eyes flamed as she drew and let go with the Schofield. Somehow, George's right hand Colt blazed a fraction before the Schofield and Vern caught lead in the center of the chest and fell back hitting the ground like a twenty pound sack of beans. Rance and the cowboy in the alley, made their move at the same moment that Vern hit the ground. In the next instant, George's left hand Colt put Rance to rest; within the blink of an eye, I unloaded both barrels of the 10 gauge into the cowboy in the alley, as he stepped out to shoot, cutting him nearly in half. I quickly broke open the shotgun and extracted the spent shells and replaced the right barrel with the one shell I had lift. Then, I snapped it shut with my good hand and readied myself for any other action.

I looked at George who was now facing me and noticed, he had not escaped unharmed, in the gunfight. There was blood streaming down the side of his face. Vern's shot had taken off a bit of the top of his left ear.

George just stood there looking at me; I starting walking toward him when Tim and the Deputy Sheriff, the Deputy with his six-shooter pulled, came running up the street toward us. George still had his pistols out and I had the shotgun ready.

About six feet in front of George the Deputy called out, "Drop those pistols an' throw up yer hands. Yer under arrest."

I stood beside George, facing Tim and the Deputy. "You ain't gonna arrest nobody here today. It was a fair fight and we weren't the ones in the wrong. Besides, the last time we gave up to a lawman, we ended up accused of something we didn't do, so, it just ain't gonna happen."

"You can't go murderin' folks in the streets of this town and get away with it," the Deputy said.

Tim interrupted, "I hate saying it, but, it was a fair fight Deputy. And, I think you should let this go for now. We don't need any more bloodshed."

"I appreciate yer bein' reasonable about this Tim," George said.

Tim looked at us stiff and unyielding. "Oh, don't get me wrong, you two; I have no respect for what you have done here today. You, killed my Father and my Aunt. And, when my brother James comes back from Abilene, he's gonna certainly form a posse with the Deputy here, and, hunt you down. And, I…I will be with him. It's a matter of family pride and justice."

"Ain't no honor or justice to be had in accusin' men of wrong, when they have done what they had to do," I said.

"Maybe so," said Tim, "but, I have to do what I have to do, also.

"So, you two best high tail it out of here, unless you want to gun us down too."

"We ain't never gunned anyone down, and we ain't startin' now," said George. "But, I ain't puttin' my ir'ns away until the Deputy does, Tim."

"Put it away Pete, and let this go for today," Tim said. The Deputy holstered his pistol and George did the same; I set the hammer on the shotgun.

## XIV

By noon the next day, we had a pack horse and our mounts loaded and left town; our plan was to head for Wickenburg, maybe hole-up there till spring. Fortunately, the weather wasn't too bad for traveling; blowing snow, not much accumulation, it took us about ten days to reach Wickenburg.

The town had a stage depot and had recently started to grow due to some gold findings in the area; and the fact that most of the Indian population was now confined to a reservation. There was still some trouble from renegades to the outlying settlers, that gave us some worry, but we didn't see hide nor hair of any hostiles all the while we were there.

Arriving late one afternoon, we quickly found a boarding house and a place to stow our gear and horses. The boarding house had an enjoyable and much appreciated meal that evening, after that I needed some rest; I was still recuperating from my shoulder injury. And, of course George found a saloon where he could do some gambling, drinking and make some money for our poke.

I did a little work for the blacksmith down at the livery stables throughout the winter and that helped offset the cost of boarding our animals. I had heeled up pretty good, with a minimum of stiffness. George had taken up drinking a lot when he was gambling, though it was getting harder and harder to tell whether he was sober or not. Even at that he played a good game of poker, he won a lot. I knew though, he was brooding over our situation and the loss of Lydia. And, we both were tired of running from our troubles.

We kind'a expected James, Tim and a posse to come riding in one day, but that never happened. Maybe, they thought it wasn't worth spilling anymore blood over; I just don't know.

Things went pretty smooth while we were there, that is, except for the one incident where George got stabbed one night. A slick looking, cheroot smoking, professional gambler got upset and felt George must be cheating. So, as George leaned back in his chair to call a barmaid to bring him a drink, the man reached around the table and jabbed him with a short bladed, boot knife, in the ribs. I was standing about five feet away when it happened, so I drew my pistol and cracked the hombre upside the head.

No one paid him any mind, laying on the floor, knocked out, but three or four locals quickly helped me get George over to the doctor's house.

The Doc said, 'No vital organs were hit,' so he cleaned the wound and sewed him up. The doctor suggested that George should spend the night there and that he should be up and around just fine in a couple days; and he was.

I headed back to the saloon to deal with the varmint that had stabbed George, but he had hightailed it out of town at the urging of some folks at the saloon; when he learned, he had stabbed Kid

Carrey, the man who had killed Mean Gene Green, there was no hesitation.

Spring came early, so George and me decided to head out toward Ehrenberg, where we could catch a riverboat down the Colorado, cross into California and head for the ocean.

## —Back to the present time—

"So Glenda," continues Cash, "You pretty well know the rest. We came here, got to know you and Sam; George made the deal with you to run the poker game and the faro table. We stayed here a lot longer than we expected too, because things were goin' so good, and now, it has cost George his life. Those rotten no good…why, I'll see to it, they'll pay fer what they've done."

"I'm sure you can do that Cash," says Glenda. "You just might get yourself killed doing it though. Sam's been wanting to buy me out for quite a while, you know, I like California, so why don't you and I just sell out and leave for California?"

"I'd be please to escort ya to California, but I got to do this first. They're not gonna give this up and I won't let it go until it's settled and ended."

"I was looking for you to be more than an escort," Glenda reached over and grasped Cash by the hand, "I have come to love you so, Cash."

Cash looked deep into Glenda's sincere, misty hazel eyes and says, "I surely believe I love you too. But, I don't think I could settle in or commit to anything, unless this deal is out of my life; 'specially since they've murdered George. Tomorrow this will be taken care of, one way, or the other."

Glenda, squeezes Cash's hand and says, "I understand, but it still worries me so."

"Sorry to worry ya. There's no other way; I'll take every advantage I can."

"Please do, Cash," Glenda says.

"Well, I got to go over to Bell's General Store and check out something that might just give me a bit of an edge."

Bell's General Store is at the east end of town at the end of the street; another street makes a T in the other direction and the store is across from where the two streets meet. As Cash walks down the street from the west, he notices it is hard to see the store, because of the brightness of the mid-afternoon sun in his eyes. Cash pulls his watch out of his pocket and looks at the time, it is ten minutes of two. 'Well now,' he says to himself, 'That certainly is interesting.'

Cash walks around the hitching rail and across the boardwalk into the store. Bell, who is behind the counter greets him and says, "I heard about, Kid Carrey; really sorry about it. Hope those scum get what's comin' to 'em. So, what can I do for you today?"

"Yeah, thanks Bell. I was thinkin' that I saw a, Walker Colt, in here a while back. You still got it?"

"Well, yeah," says Bell. "But, you don't want that old shooter. Now, I can make you a real deal on a more modern model, like a Colt New Army, got a bone handle, nickel plated, it's just like new."

"Nope, just inherited two of'm, my old .44 suits me just fine. I want that Walker, and if you got a loader outfit, I want that too."

Bell goes to a display case at the end of the counter and kneels down on the floor and opens a slid door on the bottom. He reaches in and pulls out a dark wood box and sets it on the counter. He opens the box to reveal an ornately scrolled, blue steel, Walker Colt with a walnut grip. Also, in the box is a powder flask and a collection of balls and caps. "Well, what do you think, is this what you're a looking for?"

As Cash removes it from the box, examines it and works the action on the big pistol, he says, "It's a real good piece. This is exactly, what I want. How much you want fer it?"

"How about fifteen dollars," says Bell.

"Hell no. How about nine," counters Cash.

"NINE," whines Bell. "Tell you what, I'll take Thirteen."

"But, I will only go ten, that's it; I mean, who the hell else you gonna sell it to."

"We-l-l," says Bell hesitantly, "yeah. And, you know you're a stealin' it from me."

"Well, in that case, you can have it back when I am done with it."

"You're gonna use it to deal with those hombres who murdered Kid Carrey, ain't you?"

"Yep, plain and simple," answers Cash.

"Still think you'd be better off with a second shooter like the .45 stuck in your belt," says Bell.

"Mabee so, Bell. But, I got me a plan." Cash pulls a small pouch off his belt and opens the draw string, takes out two five dollar gold pieces and drops them into Bell's palm.

Bell raises a curious brow, "What's your plan?"

Cash turns to leave with the Walker box under his arm, "Won't say fer now," he replies, "But, I'm sure you'll have the best seat in the house. Just stay away from yer front window around this time tomorrow."

Cash saddles up down at the livery stables and rides a mile or so from town. He finds a suitable hillside where he can put the big pistol to the test at about seventy to a hundred yards away. The Walker, more than meets his needs and expectations.

## XV

Cash and Glenda had made previous arrangements with two Piute Indians to have a funeral pyre for George's body and then collect the remains in a small, tin lined, wooden box. So, next morning besides Cash, Glenda and the two Piute's, four other's attended the affair on a hill just outside of town; there is Sam and three working girls from the saloon. Four feet above a significant pile of dried wood is a wooden webbed layer that holds the lifeless body of George Randolph Carrey.

All are gathered together on one side of the structure; Cash nods to the Piute's and one of them soaks a rag torch with coal oil and lights it from a small camp fire they have built. Then he goes all the way around the wood pile, igniting it. Within minutes, the burning wood quickly turns into a scorching inferno, so much so, that the observers have to back off several feet.

In about fifteen minutes the layer with the body crumbles into the blazing pile of wood and is consumed by intense flames. The two Indians start a low toned chant as the fire does its work. Cash bows his head and says, "Rest in peace ol' pard."

Glenda adds in a low tone, "Amen." Not much else is said by anyone.

They all turn to leave and Cash goes over and speaks with the Piute's, "Bring it to the saloon and give it to Sam when you're done, please." The Indians nod a solemn response.

A few hours later Cash has just finish cleaning his two pistols, he carefully lays the Walker Colt in its box and shuts it. Then, he loads his .44 with new cartridges, checks the action and spins the cylinder before planting it firmly at his side. He then tucks the Walker box under his arm and leaves the room and descends the stairs into the bar room.

Sam says as Cash walks by, "I know you gotta do this Cash, but watch yourself. Those two won't mind ambushing you and shooting you in the back."

"Thanks Sam, I appreciate the warnin'. When they come askin', tell 'em, I'll be down in front of Bell's General Store."

"Sure Cash, and I'll be watching with my shot gun ready, but, I won't interfere unless it goes bad and you need it."

"That'll be fine, and I do thank you for stayin' out'ta this; cause it's between me and them."

Glenda appears at the bottom of the stairs. "Cash," she calls and runs to him and throws her arms around his neck. She says in his ear, "You don't have to do this. I will get you the best lawyer money can buy and we'll fight this thing out."

"No, sorry Glenda, the killin' and back shootin's gone way too far for that now. This is the only way it can be settled and it's gonna end today."

"Oh Cash, I wish you wouldn't. I don't know what I will do, if I lose you."

"Don't put me in the grave quite yet, I got me a plan, and, I do know how to handle myself. This ain't my first time in a scrape."

"Well.., You come back to me; do you hear me Cash? You come back to me."

"I plan on it. Got to go now." Cash reaches around Glenda's waste, pulls her close, and kisses her passionately; he gives her a wink, and leaves the saloon and heads toward Bell's store.

On the way, Cash pulls his watch and checks the time; half past one. He takes note that the sun is just behind the top of the false front of Bell's store building. When he arrives at the store, he positions himself on the boardwalk behind the hitching rail, facing West. He pulls over a rocking chair, that is sitting on the porch, and sets down. After placing the Walker box on the boardwalk beside the chair, Cash opens it and removes the large bore pistol. He then proceeds, to load the cylinders, rams them, and puts the caps in place, readying the Walker for action. He scoots the chair up to the hitching rail and rests the Walker on the cross beam and sights it down the length of the street. "Hmm," he says, "Yep, I think that'll do just fine." He leans back in the rocking chair and lays the big pistol across his lap.

It is not long before what Cash has been longing to settle finally appears; Lambert and Ned Cromwell, come riding in to town. The two men stop in front of the saloon, Ned dismounts and goes inside, where no doubt, Sam informs him of where Cash is waiting. A minute or so later, Ned comes back out and walks up to Lambert, who is still mounted. They have a brief conversation and Ned points down the street toward where Cash is waiting. Lambert looks Cash's way down the street. He slowly dismounts and stands observing where he can barely make out the outline of his prey. He then, reaches across with his left hand and draws out his .45 Colt and checks the load and action carefully. Instead, of putting it back in place, as one might expect, he cocks the hammer back with the second joint of his thumb, relaxes his arm to his left side, with the finely tooled pistol in his hand, ready for quick reaction. Lambert, taps the trigger guard with his finger; his cold, dark blue eyes flash and the sinister smile of his, forms to fill his face with deadly anticipation. He nods down the street, "Let's get this done Ned," he says as he takes a determined step forward toward where Cash is waiting.

Ned pulls his rifle from the scabbard on his horse, and levers a cartridge into place. Ned carries it in front of him as he steps up to join Lambert's pace, and, the two walk side by side toward Cash's position.

When Lambert and Ned are within a hundred yards away, Cash leans forward and braces the Walker on the cross rail and puts Lambert in the sights. "Lambert," he yells, "Yer a back shootin', cowardly, yellow cur dog of a man. And, yer gonna pay for it today." Cash keeps him in his sights and draws back the hammer on the old Colt, slowly.

Without missing a step Lambert answer back, "And you and that no-good dead cousin of yers are murdering, no-count thieves."

Cash's mind, races through the events of the past three years, and stops on the funeral pier, as

George's body falls into the eternal flames. Lambert and Ned, are about sixty yards away now, and Cash aims, as he slowly squeezes the trigger of the Walker. Suddenly—it cracks, and echoes like a rifle shot, and sends a ball into Lambert left eye, blowing out the back of his skull. He collapses back onto the dusty street, motionless, as blood oozes out of his head.

Ned stops frozen, like a statue in the street. Cash, now stands up and lays the Walker in the rocking chair. Then, he steps around the hitching rail and walks toward Ned Cromwell. As he closes the gap between him and Ned, he adjusts his gunbelt in readiness. Ned, remains still as death, as Cash stops about six feet in front of him. "Drop that damned rifle in the dirt, Ned," orders Cash.

Ned comes back alive and says, "Shore, Cash," as he lets go of the rifle and it falls to the ground. He wrinkles up his face and pleads, "Please, don't kill me Cash."

"Oh, I could shore enough do it, but, I'm not like the rest 'a you varmints," says Cash as he walks up and back hands Ned across the face. Ned, stumbles back a step.

"So Ned," Cash says, "you got two choices. You ken either, draw that smoke wagon, in yer belt and go to work, or, just turn around and leave with yer tail between yer legs; and, don't let our paths ever cross again."

"I'll leave Cash, fer shore. And, you'll never see me again."

"Good damned deal; then get gone."

Ned, makes a half turn as if to leave, but embarrassment, has shamed up some of his nerve, so, he goes for his pistol. Cash however, anticipates his move, and, Ned turns into a .45 bullet in the chest. Now, he joins, Lambert in the street, in a puff of dust as he hits the ground. His last wrenching words are, "It weren't s'pose to end like this."

"But it did, ya damned fool," says Cash.

Glenda, pushes by Sam, who is standing in the saloon doorway with his double barrel shotgun. She runs to Cash, "CASH—Cash," she calls as she throws her arms around his neck.

Two weeks later, after Glenda had sold her share of the Saloon to her partner Sam, for a good price, and Cash had made arrangements, for the bodies of the Cromwell boy's, to be sent back to their mother in Saw Jaw, along with a letter of explanation for their deaths; the two of them are on a steamer headed down Colorado River. Cash and Glenda's plan is to get off in Yuma and go to Southern California and invest in some kind of business together.

Eighteen months later, finds Cash and Glenda at a beach front layover and saloon, they had bought. It had been a boarding house, located between Los Angeles and San Diego. Cash and Glenda transformed it into a hotel with a saloon and a dining room downstairs. Early, one sunny afternoon, Cash and Glenda, hire a boat to take them out past the breakers; they have the wooden, tin lined box with George's remains with it. When they get to calm sea, they had the skipper stop the boat, and Cash opens the box and pours out the ashes on the surface of the water, as he does, he says, "Rest in peace cousin, my ol' pard, and enjoy the ocean from now on."

A couple of days later, a letter arrived from Saw Jaw, Oklahoma; it was from Sheriff Brown, it read:

Mister Cashes De White,

It was a righteous thing for you to do, sending the bodies back here. I would have communicated with you before now had I known where to send the message. About four months ago one of Ned and Lester's old pals, Clem Hutchison was laying on his death bed from an infection caused by a rattle snake bite and wanted to clear his conscience with the Lord. He explained to me that the whole story Ned and Lester had told was a lie. That they saw nothing from the saloon that day and that Ned had told them all to back his story or they would be sorry if they didn't. Seemed to me he was really remorseful. When the bodies of Ned and Lester arrived, I went and talked to Tex McGinnis. When I told him Ned and Lester were dead, he fessed up, and told me the same story as Clem. When the bank was audited, there was a three-thousand dollar shortage on the books after the money from the robbery was added back. That was the exact amount in the saddle bags that I had confiscated from you boy's that day. So, as far as me and the Circuit Judge are concerned, you and Carrey are completely exonerated of all charges. I am truly very sorry that this didn't come to light before Mister Carrey was murdered. My sincere condolences. And, to bring this horrible mess to a conclusion, if you will forward me a bank you want me to wire the three-thousand dollars to, I will do so promptly.

I tried to reason with Misses Cromwell and tried to make her understand, but she would have no part of it.

Sincerely,
Sheriff A. Woods

After the money arrived into a Las Angeles bank, Cash and Glenda married. They both lived a very prosperous and happy life together, until their deaths. Cash died first in 1936, and Glenda followed two years later.

## THE END

Made in the USA
Charleston, SC
31 August 2016